MISSION DRAGON

This edition published in 2016 by Ipso Books

Ipso Books is a division of Peters Fraser + Dunlop Ltd

Drury House, 34-43 Russell Street, London WC2B 5HA

To young, budding conservationists, all over the world.
Together let's protect our planet and her wildlife, and
preserve our future for generations to come.

Tusk.org

CHARACTER PROFILES

Beck Granger

Beck Granger is just fourteen but knows more about the art of survival than most adults learn in a lifetime. As a small child, he picked up many traditional survival skills from the remote tribes around the world that his parents stayed with. Since then he has practiced and polished his abilities in tropical jungles, arid deserts and frozen wastes all over the globe.

Li Ju-Long

Thirteen-year-old Ju-Long has badges of excellence from her Young Pioneers battalion for sports that include camping, climbing, sailing and swimming, but she has learned the hard way that there is nothing like real experience to push you to your limits. Her ability to keep a cool head when the world is collapsing around her could be invaluable to her and to her friends.

Zhou Jian

At eighteen, Jian is already an accomplished sailor who knows the waters of the Zhujiang river and the south China coast like the back of his hand. A loyal friend, he has inherited from his father a quiet determination to see himself through hard times, and he is coolly confident – perhaps a bit *too* confident – in his abilities.

MISSION DRAGON

BEAR GRYLLS

ipso books

CHAPTER 1

Scritch. *Scritch. Scritch.*

The sound cut through the early light of dawn.

The knife was sharper than it had ever been, and Beck Granger had to make it sharper still. He would stroke the edge along a stone, over and over again, and from time to time he tested it, grim-faced, running his thumb sideways across the cutting surface. Every time he felt a little more resistance, which meant it was a little sharper.

He had always looked after his knife. It was an old friend and it had served him well. It was a simple design – the handle shaped for his hand, with a couple of folding blades, one with a sharp point and edge for cutting, and one with a jagged blade for sawing. He had used it to cut wood, to catch food, to kill and butcher animals. It had originally been his grandfather's in World War 2, handed down to his father, who in turn had given it to Beck as a young boy. It was a tool that always did exactly as Beck asked of it.

He had always kept the blades sharp. But now it had to cut more finely than a razor.

They had laid the unconscious patient on a rough mattress of netting, with chest, waist and legs tied firmly to a simple rectangular frame of wood. With no anaesthetic, they couldn't take the risk of a sudden awakening and thrashing around in the middle of the operation.

When the blade was about as sharp as it was getting, Beck sterilised it in the fire, scorching off the bacteria on the surface. With that done, he flicked out the knife's second blade, the one with the serrated edge, and sterilised that too.

"Okay," he said, when he could put it off no longer – and tried again when no sound came out. His throat was dry. He took a swig from a water bottle.

"Okay," he said again. "Let's do it."

There was light to see by, they had cut and boiled all the bandages they could, the knife wouldn't get any sharper or more sterile – and every extra minute just brought the patient a little closer to dying.

For the first time in his life, Beck had to perform surgery on another human being.

Or else, his friend would die. It was as simple as that.

He put the edge of the blade to the skin, and began to cut.

CHAPTER 2

Two days earlier

"**B**eck! Look out!"

Beck was in the bows; Li Ju-Long was at the wheel, at the other end of the boat. He just had time to see the alarm stamped all over her face, and to hear her shout.

As his head whipped round, he felt the deck pitch down beneath him.

A wall of water almost as tall as him was rising up right in front of him. He flung his arms around the forestay of the yacht, the steel cable that ran from the point of the bows to the top of the mast, and clung on for dear life as the boat cut into the wall of water. It shuddered as it hit, and foam and spray flew past his head.

"*Yee-hah!*"

He couldn't help it. He whooped.

The wave passed beneath them and the yacht rose up, then plunged down again into the dip after it. Water foamed away on either side of the bows, but this time none came on board. They were through the worst of it. Beck could finally do what he had come forward to do in the first place – free up the foresail.

Dolphin was a modern thirty foot yacht with roller reefing, which meant the foresail was rolled up around the forestay. To haul it up, someone in the cockpit just pulled on a rope attached to the clew, the free corner at the bottom, and the sail unrolled.

But it had to be released first. Now the yacht wasn't trying to throw him into the ocean, Beck could undo the plastic tie in a second, quickly and efficiently. He tucked it into his pocket and waved a hand at Zhou Jian, *Dolphin*'s young skipper, who waited at the front of the cockpit for the signal. The lanky, grinning teenager nodded and hauled back on the rope. Jian obviously loved the sea and appeared totally at ease as captain of this small yacht for the day trip. The foresail slowly unfurled, crackling and snapping at them as the canvas filled with air. Jian wound rapidly on a winch to tighten it against the wind.

They had already hauled up *Dolphin*'s mainsail and the yacht was leaning over in the steady breeze. Beck felt the difference in the yacht's motion as he picked his way back to the cockpit. They had motored out of harbour at first light with the diesel engine, and *Dolphin* had just moved like any boat, pushed by its propeller. When they put the mainsail up, the yacht had started to lean over and to protest. The engine wanted it to go one way while the wind hitting that broad expanse of canvas had had other ideas. But now, with both sails up and biting into the wind, a new thing happened. The sails were no longer in the wind's way. The boat moved *with* the wind, gracefully and easily, doing what it was designed to do.

Jian cut the engine and the transformation was complete. The vibrations died away and Beck's ears were full of the sound of wind and rushing water. *Dolphin* leaned over at about twenty degrees under the force of the wind and moved through the water as naturally as the animal it was named after. They were sailing.

"Awesome..." Beck breathed.

So much of what he did as a survivor meant working with your environment, not against it. Using what the planet gave you but not taking anything from it. The wind came because all of planet Earth's atmosphere was in constant motion, and here they were using it to get from A to B without the planet even noticing. It felt so *right*.

The day was sunny, with a stiff breeze blowing over blue, sparkling water. The mainland of China was receding behind them. It was a far cry from a week ago, when the sky had been dark and the waves churned by the hundred-mile-per-hour winds of Typhoon Liling. Beck had seen news reports showing this stretch of water, the twenty-kilometre-wide Zhujiang river estuary between the ports of Macau and Hong Kong, and was very glad to have been on land. Now, despite the wind, it was warm enough for them all to be dressed very simply: sweat tops, light trousers and deck shoes – comfortable leather slip-ons designed to get a good grip on a wet deck. They also had dark glasses and peaked caps to keep the glare out of their eyes. Jian had made them attach their caps to their bodies with loose loops of string around the neck, for those inevitable moments when the wind flipped them off.

"That was wild!" Beck shouted happily as he clambered back into the cockpit.

"I'm sorry about the wave, Beck," Ju-Long said. She looked torn between a genuine apology, and the same exhilaration he had felt as the yacht bucked beneath them. Beck hadn't exaggerated – it *had* been wild.

The red flag of China flew proudly from the stern behind her, and she never quite took her eyes off the horizon. Ju-Long was a slender girl of almost fourteen, just a little younger than him. She and Beck had met as junior leaders with the International Youth Trek Organisation only the previous week, then unexpectedly had to learn to trust and rely on each other without question when a landslide had left their trekking party stranded on a ledge high up a cliff face. They had been the only ones on the other side of the landslide, which meant that only they could climb to safety and go for help. It had meant twenty four hours of trekking through the jungles of Guangxi province, surviving thanks to Beck's skills, while the expedition's ledge slowly crumbled beneath their feet. But they had got help, and the rescuers had been able to get everyone off the ledge with only seconds to spare. A few minutes later, quite literally, and it would have been too late to save anyone.

"Hey, no worries," Beck said equably.

"It wasn't your fault, Ju-Long," said Jian, still laughing. "Blame him."

He pointed at a giant, dirty ore freighter half a mile away. The water foamed at its bow in a wave that was three metres high. *Dolphin* had been caught in its wake.

There were other boats about, of all shapes and sizes. Crammed between two busy ports, the estuary was a busy place. Beck could probably see thirty or more vessels without moving his head. The largest were a couple of massive tankers that made him think of floating skyscrapers moving horizontally through the water. They were so heavy that they would hardly notice the largest waves. They could ride as smoothly as if they were on hidden rails.

Then there were other ships – liners and freighters and fishermen – all the way down to small fry like *Dolphin*, which was just large enough for a small main cabin, a smaller forecabin, and a cockpit at the stern. The boat could probably sleep five people if it had to, though this was just a day trip.

Jian, their captain, was older than either of them – Beck guessed maybe eighteen or nineteen – but very easy to get on with, and determined to show his gratitude. His father, Mr Zhou, had been the adult left in charge of the stranded expedition, after the landslide killed its leader. Mr Zhou knew better than anyone else how close the expedition had come to disaster, and he had made sure Jian knew it too. They were both eternally grateful to Beck and Ju-Long.

There was a delay in the next stage of the expedition after the accident, because some of the authorities thought that not only should it be cancelled altogether but the International Youth Trek Organisation should be wrapped up. The members had been put up in a hotel while it all got sorted out, but Mr Zhou had insisted that Ju-Long and Beck themselves should come and stay in his own home. Beck had checked with his Uncle Al, back home in England, and Al had been happy to allow it. It wasn't just that he wanted Beck to have a holiday – he also wanted the IYTO to continue, and so he didn't want Mr Zhou to have any distractions.

And the Zhou family had *Dolphin*, the pride and joy of father and son. Jian was a trained yachtsman and had been sailing all his life. When Mr Zhou was called up to head office, Jian had asked if they could take the yacht out to pass the time. And here they were.

"So, where are we going?" Beck asked. He and Ju-Long had been Junior Leaders with IYTO, and he had ended up leading an emergency expedition down the river. Now he was perfectly happy to let someone else be in charge.

Jian ducked quickly into the cabin, and came up again with a chart which he unfurled on the cabin roof. Unlike a normal map, which showed rivers and roads and hills and towns, the land on this was just a single blank shade. It was the sea that had all the differences, with different colours showing the range of depths and currents and obstacles.

"Somewhere with fewer ships. Down here."

He tapped the bottom of the chart. Small, irregular shapes were scattered across the bottom, from the size of a large coin to little specks of ink.

"This is the archipelago," Jian said. "You can see the islands are all kinds of sizes. Tourists enjoy the bigger ones." He waved a finger over the larger blobs at the eastern end. "But we are going this way." Now he showed the smaller specks to the west. "Most of them are uninhabited and it is too shallow for the larger ships – so, nice and solitary. We will have a good day's sail and be back home in time for dinner!"

It was obvious from his smile that to him 'a good day's sail' was the best thing anyone could hope for. His enthusiasm and his love of the sport were infectious.

"Well," Beck said with a grin. He lounged on one of the benches and stretched his arms out on either side of the cockpit coaming. "No hurry!"

No hurry at all, he thought.

Back home in Britain, he had made a bit of a name for himself. He had never wanted it – it had just sort of happened. There were upsides, and he tried to use it to push the messages and the values that he believed in, which matched those of organisations like IYTO – but it was also a pain when some magazine called asking for a comment or opinion about some boy band or YouTube sensation that he had never heard of. He was learning how to positively say no.

Coming to China was meant to have been a break from all that, and it had been – right up until everything went sideways on the expedition.

Maybe now, just for one day, he could sit back and enjoy letting the wind do all the work...

CHAPTER 3

Beck's fingers closed over the rim of the steering wheel and he stared fixedly at the compass, which bobbed inside a small glass dome in front of him. The boat was drifting slightly off its course so he turned the wheel to compensate. *Dolphin* started to turn but quickly overshot, so Beck turned the wheel back the other way.

"Do not be..." Jian paused. "I do not know the English word. Do not be..."

He crossed his eyes and waved his fingers in front of Beck's face, like a stage magician performing a trick.

Beck laughed nervously.

"Hypnotised?"

"Hypnotised. Okay. Do not be hypnotised by the compass. There is a right way and a wrong way," Jian went on happily. "The wrong way is to move the wheel a little every time we go a little off course. The right way – look at the sails, look at the horizon."

Beck looked up.

"The compass can only give you the general direction. You have to *feel* the boat's direction, and you make small corrections all the time – so small you barely notice."

"You will barely notice you are doing it," Ju-Long predicted with a smile. She had already gone through the training.

"Okay..."

Beck reluctantly tore his eyes from the compass. He kept them on the horizon and concentrated.

And soon found that Jian was absolutely right. Keeping course became as easy as walking, if you just felt the boat as an extension of your body, and moved the wheel accordingly. When he glanced back, he saw that the wake was smooth and straight, showing that *Dolphin* was cutting a steady, straight line through the water.

In many ways it went against his own training – he was used to keeping course as exactly as possible on land, because even a small error at first could accumulate into a very big error later on. With a sailing boat, different rules counted.

But he was in the hands of Jian, an expert, and he loved to learn new stuff about how things worked. So he relaxed, and enjoyed it, and learnt a new skill.

They sailed on through the morning, averaging between six and nine knots – seven and ten miles per hour. Beck was surprised at how quickly the mainland grew slowly smaller behind them. Another thing about a sailing boat was that it might not move fast – but it kept moving, never needing a rest or a break, as long as the wind was blowing.

Jian seemed constantly on the move – checking the trim of the sails, taking over the wheel for a few moments so that he could feel the way *Dolphin* handled. It was still relaxing for Beck and Ju-Long – unhurried, with the feeling of being in competent hands. Jian also made them tell the full story of their expedition down the gorge, and how they had saved his father's life. That led on to Beck having to tell them about his other adventures – which he had never enjoyed having to do, but he couldn't really get out of it.

As the shipping lanes drew further behind them, the small islands of the archipelago began to emerge from the sea haze in front. The sun beat down and would have been quite merciless without cover. There was a small awning over the wheel for who-ever was steering, and the other two just had to shelter behind their hats or under a layer of sun cream. Beck was glad he had chosen long trousers and shirt sleeves. Before they set off, he had wondered if he should face the day in shorts and t-shirt. If he had stayed on land then he probably would. But, out here, the effect of sun and wind and salt spray on bare skin would have been like scraping it with a grater.

They could have gone into the cabin, of course – but where would the fun be in that? The point of sailing, Beck thought, was to sail – to be part of the boat and the sea and the wind. Outside.

At first the islands were just dark splodges on the horizon. It was impossible to get an idea of their shape, or tell which ones were big and far away, or small and close by. Jian knew these waters like the back of his hand and kept them on a steady south-south-west course.

The dark blobs began to stretch out and separate as they kept going, like a piece of putty breaking into pieces as someone pulled on it. The shape of the archipelago was becoming clearer. Beck always liked to know where he was, so he retrieved the chart and matched what it showed with what he could see.

None of the cluster of small islands at the end of the archipel-ago, where they were heading, was more than a quarter of a mile or so across. Jian was going to take them anti-clockwise around the very last one in the group. Then they would come back down a channel between the last island and the second last one, and sail back to the mainland.

The chart had plenty of rocks and shoals marked on it. Some would be visible, some would be underwater, depending on the tide, but Jian knew them all.

"This channel is completely safe," he said, tapping the space between the islands. "And we can drop anchor here and have our lunch."

It was Beck's turn to be at the wheel again as the last island drew near. They passed it by on the port side – the left. It reminded him of a fortress built in the sea. There were no sandy beaches to lounge about on. Most of it seemed to be a platform of boulders and rocks that were only just higher than the sea they rose out of. Even now, the sea rose and fell so that the rocks were covered in a thin layer of water that was always in motion. It was either washing in with the next wave, or it was draining out again through the nooks and crannies. Then the next wave would come in and start the process all over again.

The centre of the island was a little higher, basically a big lump of rock, with a thin layer of soil that had accumulated over the centuries on the bits that the tide didn't reach. It was covered thickly in foliage, where seeds had blown over from the mainland and taken root in soil that was just thick enough to support them. So, everything would be battling for height and ground, without anything being able to get really massive. It was wild and untamed, all jumbled together without any human hand to guide it.

Beck could also see the damage that the recent typhoon had caused. It must have smashed through here like an express train. Many trees lay uprooted, and bushes were still pressed flat against the ground. They were just starting to straighten up again. Without anywhere to shelter, the islands would not have been pleasant places to be.

"Beck!" Jian called. He was standing on the foredeck, legs apart to brace himself. He pointed to starboard, to the right, with a flat hand to indicate that Beck should steer a little more away from the island. Beck nodded and turned the wheel a fraction until Jian was satisfied. Ju-Long tightened one of the winches to adjust the sails to the new direction. With the island to one side, there was now no land at all ahead until – well, Beck thought, probably Indonesia. And that was a good two thousand kilometres away. It was like they were at the very end of China.

"Thank you." Jian began to come back to the cockpit. "A wind like this could blow us onto the shore so it is best to keep distance –"

CRASH.

Dolphin stopped as abruptly as if it had run into a brick wall. The vibration ran through the entire boat and the sound of splintering fibreglass came up through the cabin hatch.

Jian was flung down onto one side. He landed awkwardly on his left arm with a shout of pain. The rim of the wheel banged into Beck's ribs as an invisible force threw him forwards. Ju-Long, who was sitting on one of the cockpit benches, was flung to the floor like a rag doll.

Then, suddenly, *Dolphin* was moving again. It was turning, towards the island, blown around by the wind. Beck spun the wheel but it didn't make any difference.

"Jian?" he shouted. Jian was slowly trying to sit up, clumsily, thwarted by the boat's random movement. His left arm seemed dead, and he was clutching it hard with his right hand, which meant he didn't have a hand to spare for himself. His teeth were clamped, his face set in a mask of pain.

There was something strange about the yacht's motion, Beck realised. It no longer cut through the waves. It seemed to be bobbing on top, like a toy in the bathtub, not like a proper boat. And it wasn't moving forward.

But it was leaning. It always leaned away from the wind, a little, but now it was more and more over, to port. The left side of the boat was dipping down into the sea. Thirty degrees. Forty. Forty five. From the cabin came the sound of things dropping and breaking.

Then it was more than halfway over. Beck braced himself against the increasing angle and watched with horror as the sea came closer and closer to the edge of the cockpit.

CHAPTER 4

J ian had struggled into a sitting position. He began to call their names, then broke off as his face contorted in pain and he clutched his arm again. He finished the sentence in a spurt of Chinese.

"He says, we must get the sails down. He thinks the keel has gone," Ju-Long translated, as she scrambled up out of the cockpit. Beck quickly scrabbled his way up to help her. *Dolphin*'s rudder was almost out of the water, so abandoning the wheel made no difference. The boat was so far over that the three of them were standing or sitting on the starboard side of the cabin.

And Beck could see at once that Jian was right. There was just a jagged hole in the fibreglass hull where the keel should have been, and water lapped against the broken edges.

Without the weight of the keel underneath, the force of the wind in the sails was enough to blow the yacht over. And that was why they weren't moving. A sailing boat moved forwards because it was balanced between the pressures on the sails and the keel. But with no keel...

They had to get the sails down before *Dolphin* was knocked completely flat.

Jian muttered something else, almost to himself.

"And he thinks he has broken his arm," Ju-Long added.

And I think he's right about that, too, Beck thought grimly. He could see the way Jian's arm was hanging. When the older boy had fallen over, he had landed even more badly than it looked.

"I would help if I could –" Jian mumbled, now in English. He scooted on his backside away from the mast, still holding his arm, to make room for Beck and Ju-Long.

"Don't worry about it. First things first," Beck assured him quickly. He released the halyard for the mainsail and pulled it down with strong, steady heaves, while Ju-Long took care of the foresail.

But the port side of the cockpit had reached the level of the sea. Water splashed over it, then began to pour in as the boat settled further. The cabin hatch was still above the water, but somehow Beck could hear the sound of water gurgling inside the cabin. He crawled along the side of the boat to peer through the hatch, and cursed under his breath at what he saw.

They had opened the cabin windows to get fresh air into the boat. Now the port side windows were below water and it was gushing in, its weight dragging *Dolphin* down even further. Even as Beck watched, the water reached the open hatch.

"It's going down!" Jian called. "It's too late to save it!"

CHAPTER 5

Going down.

Caught on a sinking boat, every particle of Beck's body wanted to leap off. But common sense told him it still had a few minutes left, and maybe he could do something to help? No survivor ever achieved anything by panicking. You had to stay on top of the situation.

What had they hit? he wondered. Jian had been so confident, and then – *crash.* But that wasn't important right now. Survive this, and they would have all the time they wanted to ask why.

His eyes fixed on a pair of life buoys tied to the stern rail, fastened with knots that could be released with a couple of tugs. They were shaped like giant letter 'U's, made of plastic-covered foam. Okay, those would be needed. He jumped down into the flooded cockpit and stood on what used to be the doors of the side lockers beneath the benches, so that the water came up to his knees. He pulled the life buoys free and carried them with him as he clambered back up onto the side of the yacht.

Ju-Long was speaking rapidly to Jian in Chinese, with gestures at the water. Jian nodded. Ju-Long knelt and pushed her face into the water while she fumbled with something below the surface. Jian waited, seething with impatience and his useless arm.

"She is trying to get the life raft," he said by way of explanation to Beck, and Beck understood. The raft was in a hard plastic shell the size of a water barrel, tied to the roof of the cabin. Once it was released it would open up and inflate itself automatically.

But the buckles that fastened the straps were on the other side of the boat – underwater. Ju-Long reared her head up suddenly, with water streaming from her face. She gasped, took a deep breath and plunged herself back under before either Beck or Jian could say anything. She would be doing it all by feel – Beck knew what it was like trying to see underwater without a mask, with the salt turning your eyes raw. It was next to impossible. But he also knew she wouldn't stop trying. She was never one to panic – she analysed what was needed, with a cool head, and went for it. In the jungle she had been the first one to say out loud that they had to go for help. Her first thought was always for how she could help others.

The sea washed over his shoes. They still stood on the side of the cabin and almost all the boat was under. Ju-Long suddenly brought her head up again, gasping for breath.

"I can't reach …"

"Never mind," Beck said quickly, grabbing her before she went back for a third, futile effort. He cocked an eye at the island – it couldn't be more than a hundred metres away. "We can swim it – right, Jian?"

Jian was the captain and the final decision to abandon ship had to be his. Jian gazed helplessly at the island, and at the boat sinking beneath his feet, and nodded without speaking.

"Here …" Beck said. He pushed one of the U-shaped life buoys under Jian's armpits. The older boy hissed with pain as he was forced to raise his broken arm up, but then it was done.

"Just lie down," Beck said, giving him a gentle push to back up his words. Jian struggled to resist at first, until he realised what Beck was doing. He sat back and the buoy simply floated him off *Dolphin*'s hull.

Beck chucked the other buoy into the water, and he and Ju-Long dived in after it. If he had been wearing anything bulky then he would have stripped it off first, but the clothes and shoes he had were light enough not to matter. What counted was getting off the boat before it took them down with it.

The water was cool – under any other circumstances it would have been refreshing. They popped up beside Jian and grabbed hold of the buoy between them. They trod water and turned to look back at the yacht.

Heavy bubbles heaved around the sinking boat. By now, only the tip of the mast – the crosstrees that jutted out on either side, and the radar reflector – stuck out of the water, not quite level with the surface. The angle of the mast slowly grew steeper again as the boat sank beneath it. It stopped moving with about three metres showing, sticking up at an angle that was about twenty degrees off the vertical. *Dolphin* must have settled on the bottom at a depth of about ten metres.

Jian was still in a daze, staring at the top of the mast. Ju-Long and Beck, not feeling much better, clung onto their buoy and gazed at where the yacht had been.

Concentrate, concentrate, Beck told himself. It wasn't the first time calamity had struck suddenly. He made himself run through the options in his head.

There was a radio in the cabin, but everything had happened too quickly to send off a distress call. And there were distress flares in the cockpit lockers which could have been used to get the attention of rescuers – but, again, too quickly. Even if they could dive down to the boat – he would have to think about that – the radio would be useless by now. The flares, probably not so much. They were in sealed metal tubes, watertight. If he could get at them.

He glanced over at the island. It had looked closer when he was still on the boat. At sea level, with his eyes only a couple of inches above the water, it looked a lot further. But it was where they had to be. It was so close that it was the obvious destination to get to, and they should do it before the tide turned and swept them away.

"Let's get moving," he said. Ju-Long nodded, and spoke to Jian in Chinese. Then she said it again, more sharply to get his attention. He seemed to snap back into the real world.

"Can you swim?" Beck asked. Jian's face was taut and pale, and he still held his teeth together unless he absolutely had to say something. But he nodded.

"I still have legs."

"Okay ... Hang on ..."

There were rope handles around the edges of the buoys so that multiple survivors could hang onto each one. Beck untoggled one from his buoy, threaded it through a handle on Jian's, and reattached it to his own. Now the two buoys were linked and no one would be left behind.

"Let's go, then."

Jian gave a last look back at the tip of the mast, still poking bravely above the waves. Then he started to kick his away from the wreck with firm thrusts of his legs. His face was set in agony but he never made a sound.

It took a long time for the island to draw near. Salt water splashed against Beck's face and into his eyes. He could feel the surges of the waves through the water, half the time pulling them closer to the island, half the time pushing them back, so that it felt like they were making no progress at all. The steep sides that Beck had seen from the boat looked even harsher from surface level, and the island towered out of the water above them.

But, over the sound of their splashing feet, Beck's ears picked up the sound of water hitting rocks. They were drawing closer, bit by bit, and he could feel the invisible force of the swell, picking him up and letting him down again. He craned his neck, trying to make himself as high up as he could to get a better view of what lay ahead, and saw a wave dashing itself into foaming pieces on the boulders around the island's base. He remembered the layers of rocks and boulders. They would be harsh and unforgiving. They could tear the bottom of a boat out, just as easily as break bones.

He saw the look of calculation on Jian's face – the grim set to the older boy's jaw as he squared up to the near certainty of his broken arm bashing against the rocks, and a lot more pain.

"Okay," Beck said grimly. "We're going to have to time this just right ..."

Even as he spoke, he felt the next wave lifting them up and towards the island.

CHAPTER 6

Beck fixed his eyes on the rocks ahead, calculating by pure instinct.

"And – *swim!*"

They kicked furiously, propelling themselves forward. Up ahead, the wave disintegrated into foam as it dashed against the rocks, and now they were heading straight for a hard, jagged boulder crusted with barnacles. White water surged around them. It reminded Beck too vividly of his recent adventure in the jungle, when he had inadvertently been swept away by a river into rapids. The water hissed and bubbled with a life of its own.

And then, just as surely as they had felt the force carrying them towards the island, suddenly the island was pushing them away again. The waves were draining back off the rocks.

"Try and hold steady," Beck ordered. "Don't let it carry us too far away ..."

The next wave was coming in. Beck could feel its force growing beneath them.

"This is the one. *Go!*"

The wave carried them up and over the rock. A shudder ran through the life buoys as they grounded, and Beck felt his knees and legs bang and scrape against the hard surface. Jian made a sound somewhere between a grunt and a whimper.

The draining water pulled at them like a thousand little fingers, trying to pluck them back into the ocean. Beck and Ju-Long scrambled to their feet, dripping wet with their clothes plastered to their bodies, and they helped Jian stand up, while the running water made bow waves around their shins. Together they grabbed the life buoys and hurried further up the rocks.

Behind them, Beck heard the next wave crashing in – but now they were high enough up that its remnants, the very last of the foam, only splashed around their feet. A few more metres, and they could drop the life buoys.

Jian sank straight down into a squat, his head between his knees, clutching his broken wrist. Ju-Long bent double, her hands resting on her knees while she spat out the foul taste of salt water. Beck stood with his hands on his hips and drew in slow, deep breaths while he looked around.

They were on a rocky ledge that extended for thirty or forty metres in either direction, before it curved out of sight. It was pitted with small rock pools and inlets where the sea surged in and out. Beck made a mental note of the pools. If there were fish trapped in them then they would be easy picking for three shipwrecked castaways.

The ledge sloped gently upwards, away from the sea, to a small cliff a couple of metres high. The granite rocks were all shades of dark grey, while an even darker streak showed where water was trickling down from the high ground.

Between them and the cliff was a line of dead, dried seaweed and flotsam – man-made rubbish that had been washed up, then left behind when the tide went down. That was the high water mark – the highest point that the water reached when the tide came in.

Jian was muttering, very quietly, in Chinese – the same words, over and over again. Beck couldn't understand the words but he could read the tone. Harsh and bitter.

"He says, 'it's my fault, it's my fault'," Ju-Long said quietly. And again, Beck found himself wondering what had caused the accident. Jian knew these waters and he had had the chart. He wouldn't have taken the boat in close to any danger that he knew about.

But, trying to reassure Jian probably would be hard. The fact was that responsibility came down to the guy in charge. Beck didn't know if Jian could have done anything different. He couldn't tell if it really had been Jian's fault or not. What he did know was that Jian was a good sailor. He wanted to remind Jian of the things he could do well, to stop him beating himself up. That was quite apart from the medical help he was going to need to deal with that broken bone, and the shock and pain.

And a good sailor would know the tides.

So, Beck spoke, deliberately loud.

"Jian, what's the tide doing now?"

Jian looked up and took a breath.

"It's low tide right now." He still sounded dazed, bewildered, not quite able to believe he was here and having to say this now. "We were going to go around the island and the incoming tide would help carry us back to the mainland."

"Okay." Beck checked his watch – it was waterproofed to fifty metres and a small thing like a shipwreck wouldn't have affected it at all. It was just short of one p.m., and the tide worked on a cycle of just over twelve hours from low to high to low again. "So. High tide is at seven."

By sunset, the place where they were standing would be underwater. That was fine – it gave them plenty of time to explore.

Above the cliff was the rest of the island. The tightly packed undergrowth that Beck had seen from the sea came right up to the edge and, this close up, the damage caused by the recent typhoon was even more obvious. The hundred-mile-per-hour winds had torn branches away and uprooted trees, and now they were all matted together.

Jian looked back at where *Dolphin*'s mast still stuck out of the water.

"It must have been the typhoon," he said suddenly. "It tore up the sea bed as well. It disturbed the sand banks – it probably moved rocks about. The keel hit one of them. I know these waters but I didn't think they might have changed." His shoulders sagged. "I should have realised."

Ju-Long put a hand on his good shoulder.

"No one is blaming you," she said gently.

"We're here, we're alive," Beck agreed. "The big question is – how long will it be until we're missed? And will they know where to look for us?"

"How long?" Jian cocked his head as he thought. "My father was not sure how long he would be away. It could be a week or more. I asked him if I could take you out on *Dolphin*, but I did not say where, and he would not expect us to get in touch while we were on board. So, it might be a week before he misses us. Then, he might guess I headed for the archipelago but he will not know which bit."

This was bad news. Boats weren't like aeroplanes, Beck thought, where you had to file a flight plan before you took off. Then, if anything happened to you en route, rescuers would realise when you didn't turn up, and they would have a vague idea of where to look for you.

"Okay." He thought quickly. "So we might have to stay alive for a week, maybe a bit longer. If we don't get rescued first. We can do that."

Jian looked up at him sceptically and drew a breath to speak – and then let it out again.

"All those things you were telling us about," he said. "How you have survived in other places. You can do that now?"

"No," Beck said promptly. Both Ju-Long and Jian looked at him sharply, and he corrected what Jian had said. "*We* can do it now. The three of us, working together."

The last thing he wanted was for Jian to start feeling useless. Any survivor had to keep a positive attitude in their head, and the more they were injured, the harder that became. Jian was the oldest, the experienced sailor, *Dolphin*'s captain. Under any other circumstances he would have been the one in charge. Just because he had an injured hand, Beck saw no reason for him to be diminished in any way.

"Beck is right," Ju-Long chipped in. "When we were in the gorge, he was the one who knew where to find food, how to prepare a camp for the night – but I could also teach him some things."

"Yup." Beck grinned at the memory. He still remembered the awe he had felt as Ju-Long used her *ki* energy, with feats of strength and ability that Beck would have thought were impossible.

Jian looked from one of them to the other, and for the first time something like a smile flickered over his glum features.

"The three of us," he said. "That will be good."

"But first," Beck said, "let's have a look at your arm. See how bad it is."

Jian hesitated, but then he shrugged. Nothing that could happen would make it worse than it was. He sat clumsily down on the rock and rested his arm on his lap.

Beck gently took hold of it and started to roll back the sleeve, and despite his deliberate optimism he braced himself for whatever he might find.

CHAPTER 7

Jian's left arm was red and swollen and bruised, but Beck immediately breathed a sigh of relief. It was a closed fracture. The bone was broken, but it didn't penetrate the skin. That would have opened up whole new areas of complication, such as how to dress the wound, or how to stop it getting infected.

There was an especially inflamed spot a few centimetres above the wrist, which Beck knew was the break itself. Jian's arm kinked at that point, with the hand considerably out of line with the rest of it. But he knew better than to take anything for granted, especially where broken bones were concerned. And so he gently pressed his fingers against Jian's skin, starting at the shoulder and working his way down. He was feeling for swollen tissue, for muscles that spasmed – and of course for the edges of the broken bone. Just because he knew where one break was didn't mean there weren't others.

"Have either of you done a medical course in the Young Pioneers?" he asked conversationally as he went. He had gathered that Jian, like Ju-Long, had been a member of the Chinese youth organisation until he was fourteen.

"First aid," Ju-Long said.

"Nothing like…" Jian nodded at his hand.

"Okay. We need to establish exactly where the break is, and I think it's going to be – sorry, Jian – here…"

He pushed gently with his fingertips at the red spot. Jian hissed abruptly through his teeth and shuddered.

"Right." Beck sat back on his haunches and considered. He could do with some ice…

He had broken one of his own arms in the last year – but that had been in Nepal, on a snowy, icy mountain. Finding ice to put on the break and reduce the swelling hadn't been hard, there, but it wasn't going to happen here.

"I think you've got what's called a Colles fracture – a broken wrist. It's either the ulna or the radius bones, probably the radius."

And very disabling, he didn't add. Jian would find that out soon enough. Beck's medical instructor had told him how she had once driven home with a break near the elbow: it worked because the other bone acted as a splint, holding the break in place. This close to the wrist, though, the break didn't have that kind of support. She had known people faint from a Colles fracture.

"The best we can do is splint it, and try to get rescued," Beck finished.

"You can do that?" Jian asked cautiously.

"I can." Beck had practiced it many times – he didn't mention that he had never actually had to do it on a human patient.

"Then do what you have to do," Jian muttered.

Beck suppressed a shiver. They were all soaked through, and even in the sun, the wind on their wet clothes was going to chill them until they were properly dried out. They were all full of adrenaline, so they would feel colder as it drained out of them. And Jian was probably in shock, which would make him feel colder still. Beck wished they had something to wrap him up in.

But it told him what the first priority was for Jian, even before they splinted the break.

"Let's get you somewhere warm. Over here."

There was a nook in the rocks, a bit further up, beyond the high water mark. It was out of the wind, and it faced south, so the rocks were dry and warmed by the sun.

Beck and Ju-Long helped Jian to his feet. Jian looked like he was going to wave their help away, until he stumbled slightly and once again hissed through his teeth as pain lanced up and down his arm. Then he let them escort him to the nook, and help him to settle down again.

"Just rest quietly here," Beck said. "Warm up and dry out while we explore. We need to see what we've got to work with – see if we can get something to fix your arm, for a start."

Jian shot them a ghost of a smile.

Beck picked his way around the rocks at the base of the island, following the high water mark. The shoreline was always a rich hunting ground for a survivor – all kinds of goodies could be included in that flotsam. A mental map was growing inside his head: the layout of the island, and the resources they had at their disposal. It was pretty sketchy at the moment, but it would fill out with detail.

Most of the high water mark was weed, dried and twisted in the sunlight, but there was other stuff too. A dead, rotting sea bird, probably a booby – almost a skeleton, with a few strips of flesh and feathers clinging to it, and a powerful, pointed beak. A plank of wood, still with some bits of paint that had not yet been washed off. An empty plastic bottle. A length of orange plastic netting, of the type that road repair crews might use to section off some roadworks – more like a sheet of plastic with holes in it. A square lump of polystyrene foam that, to judge from the shapes cut into it, must have once been part of the packaging for something thin and electronic – maybe a laptop or a DVD player. There seemed to be a universal law, Beck thought with anger, that every shore on the planet should have at least one lump of washed-up polystyrene on it. The stuff might float extremely well but it took millions of years to degrade, and most of twenty-first century civilisation seemed to be based on it.

And there would be stuff like this all around the island. He made a mental note of where everything was. Everything could come in useful, maybe even the dead bird, though right now he couldn't quite think how.

He kept going until he came to a promontory of high ground that stuck out into the sea. The waves washed right up to its base and he couldn't go any further. He craned his head back as he looked up at it. It was ten metres high and its side was a sheer cliff. He could probably have climbed it, but at the moment his priority was finding anything that might be useful for Jian, and climbing would just take up time he could use for other purposes. It wouldn't take much longer just to go around the island the other way, until he got to the promontory on the other side.

But it was useful to know the high ground was there. He could already think of a very good use for it.

He made his way back the way he had come, this time picking up bits of flotsam as he went. It made him feel a little like a character in a kids' computer game, retrieving treasures as he progressed across an alien landscape. By the time he reached Jian's nook in the rocks, he had a small pile of planks in both arms, with the orange netting and polystyrene block balanced on top, and the bottle and a single foam flip-flop tucked into his waistband.

Ju-Long was already there, bent double beneath a fishing net that she had had to sling over her back to carry. It was big and black, tangled up into a mass the size of a very fat, tall man, crusted with weed and grit and shells.

"Wow!" Beck exclaimed. In one stroke, Ju-Long had supplied all their rope needs for the foreseeable future – considerably stronger, and considerably easier to get hold of, than the vines they had had to make do with in the river gorge.

"There is a small beach in that direction – gravel, not sand. This was washed up – and a lot of other stuff, but I thought it would be useful."

"You were right," he assured her. She had really learned the survivor's art of identifying the resources available, and using them. It was good to know he could rely on her help.

"And this," she said proudly. She gave a fold of the netting a tug, and a coconut fell out onto the rocks. Not the brown, wizened, dried out thing you would get at a fairground but the real deal, the size of a football and encased in green leaves.

"Well, you got lunch!" he said. "But first let's see what else we have."

They dumped everything into a small pile. Beck sifted through the pieces of wood until he had found a couple the right sort of length for Jian's splint. They were both straight and smooth and flat – they had been part of something, maybe a boat or a building, quite possibly smashed up and washed out to sea by the typhoon. He knocked them together experimentally. They seemed firm, not likely to snap at a moment's notice, and they were fully dried out.

He dug into his pocket for his knife – one of the two personal items that he took everywhere with him, even on sailing holidays – and began to slice off a couple of thin, flat lengths from the block of polystyrene, the same length as the bits of wood.

"Here's how it is," he said conversationally as he worked. He wanted it to sound straightforward, matter-of-fact, to help Jian relax as much as possible. "The muscles of your arm will have contracted, to try and protect the bone." He held his two forefingers out, crossed in an X. "The broken ends will be overlapping and the muscles will be holding them in place like that. Unfortunately that makes it harder to reset it, so we're going to have to apply traction. That basically means Ju-Long and I pull on it in different directions. Right?"

If he could have been sure that rescue was only a few hours away, he would have just splinted the arm as it was. The broken bone would have been held steady and it wouldn't have got any worse, until a doctor could knock Jian out with an anaesthetic and do it properly. The broken ends wouldn't grind together, and they wouldn't move around and cause damage to flesh or nerves or blood vessels.

Unfortunately, they couldn't be sure when rescue would arrive. It was safest to assume the worst, and make the arm the best it could be now.

Jian set his jaw firmly and nodded very quickly.

"Right," he said. Beck noticed his breathing was speeding up. He knew pain was coming and this was how anyone would react.

Beck shook a length out of the pile of Ju-Long's black net, and cut three short lengths of rope. The splint was almost ready. He laid the three lengths on the ground, side by side, and then rested one of the bits of driftwood on top of them, with a strip of polystyrene on top of that. Last of all, he took Jian's forearm and gently laid it on top of the polystyrene.

The time had come. He bit his lip and looked down at Jian.

"This is going to hurt," he said. Jian was pale, but resolved.

"I know. Just do it."

Beck moved his grip to Jian's elbow and nodded at Ju-Long. She gently took hold of his wrist with both hands.

"Okay. Go."

Beck clenched his fingers tight, took a deep breath, and pulled.

CHAPTER 8

Jian's face was twisted, his eyes screwed tight shut, and something like a slow scream squeezed through his clenched teeth.

Between them, Ju-Long and Beck stretched Jian's forearm out. Beck kept a steady grip on his elbow with one hand, and he kept the fingers of the other over the break. There was a sudden shift beneath the skin as the two broken ends popped back together.

Shudders ran through Jian's body as Beck grabbed the second strip of polystyrene and the second piece of wood, and quickly laid them on top of Jian's arm. Jian was making retching sounds, as though he might be about to throw up. Beck swiftly tied the ends of the rope over them and over the arm, deftly whipping them into a square knot.

Jian's shaking slowly died down. His shoulders stopped heaving. He swallowed a couple of times, still like he might be about to spew, which Beck knew would be a perfectly normal reaction to what had just happened. But after a minute, even that seemed to be under control.

"Okay." Beck pinched the ends of his fingers. "Can you feel that"?

"Yes." Jian gasped the word out as though it were on his last breath.

"Do your fingers feel cold?"

Jian shook his head and Beck puffed his cheeks out with a sigh of relief. The knots he had tied were tight enough to hold the splints in place, but not so much that they cut off the blood or the feeling to Jian's arm. The wood on either side would keep his arm steady and hold the break so that it could heal. The polystyrene was padding to prevent the wood chafing against his skin.

Beck cut off a length of the plastic netting and tied the two ends together to make a sling. He hung it around Jian's neck, then gently rested the splinted arm in it.

"How do you feel?" he asked.

"About as comfortable as anyone with a broken arm and no painkillers can be," Jian said grimly. His voice was sounding stronger and Beck smiled to himself. As long as Jian didn't take any knocks to the arm, or over-exert himself, he should be okay, for the time being.

They sat together and Beck drilled a pair of holes in the coconut with his knife – one to let the air in, one to drink from. He hoped it wasn't too obvious that he passed it to Jian first. Jian was the one who most needed it but Beck knew he wouldn't want to think he was being nursemaided.

If Jian noticed, he didn't say thing. He only took a small sip of the rich, nutritious fluid before passing it on, and that was how they finished it off – each taking turns with a small amount until it was all gone. The perfect balance of salt, minerals and sugar, Beck thought – if the coconut came from a tree on this island, then there was a good chance of finding more. There again, it could have been in the sea for months, floating hundreds of miles, hermetically sealed against the salt water and still perfectly fresh. Time would tell.

Once it was drained, he cracked the shell open with the blade and sliced out portions of the creamy white meat that lined the inside.

They all felt more human once it was all gone. It was mid-afternoon – they had missed lunch, and everything else that had happened had drained the strength from them until their bodies were crying out for something to replenish it with.

"Now I just need some water to wash it down," Ju-Long said. It was meant to be a light remark, but Jian's face suddenly grew long, the good mood that comes after a meal forgotten.

"There was plenty of fresh water in *Dolphin*'s tanks," he remarked gloomily. True, Beck thought, but not helpful. He was determined that the older boy shouldn't be allowed to dwell on the accident. Jian could spend the rest of his life kicking himself for losing *Dolphin*. That would not help them survive now.

"Well, there's water over here."

Beck walked to the base of the cliff, and the dark streak that he had noticed earlier. Closer up, he could see it was a thin, glistening film of water that dribbled slowly down the rock face. It pooled at the base of the cliff, and then trickled away to disappear into the million little cracks and crevices of the rock ledge. He put his lips to the wet rock and sucked in. Water sprayed into his mouth like a light aerosol. The rock gave it a dry, stale flavour – it was like sucking on a pebble. It wasn't thirst-quenching, but it was fresh, and it was good. He smacked his lips.

"Give it a go," he suggested. The other two both looked at him like he had gone mad.

"We live off that?" Jian asked.

"I didn't say we live off it – but we can top ourselves up."

Jian looked up at the rest of the island.

"The soil is so thin there probably won't be proper pools or streams," he said thoughtfully. "Rain water will just soak through the soil, enough to water the plant life, and come trickling out in places like this."

Yet again, Beck thought, that was true but not helpful. It would hardly be enough to keep three of them alive for long. It was ironic that they were surrounded by water. He knew it was possible to get so thirsty that you would happily chug down any liquid, but salt water would only kill you even more quickly. The salt would fry your kidneys and dehydrate you, sucking away what little good water there was in your tissues. There was only one result. Delirium, coma, and death.

"Still better than nothing," he said. "There's other ways to get water."

An adult needed three litres of water a day – and that was if they were mostly standing still, not doing much. The three of them were all close enough to adulthood that they couldn't do with much less, Jian especially – and they would not just be standing still. They would have to be active, trying to survive, fighting a hot sun and breathing air that was laced with salt spray.

Even if it only took a week to be rescued, if they didn't find water then their rescuers would only find bodies.

Ju-Long raised her eyebrows, but she came forward and pressed her mouth against the wet rock as Beck had done.

"Mm. That is good," she said as she stepped away.

"Care for some?" Beck offered to Jian with a smile. Jian frowned, then knelt and scooped a handful of water out of the small pool with his good hand. He did not get much because the pool was only about the same size as his hand in the first place.

"There were more places like this at the beach that I found," Ju-Long said. "And it is shaded by trees."

"Sounds like that might be our camp, then. That's two out of four things dealt with."

"What four things?" Jian asked.

"Protection, rescue, water, food." Beck ticked them off on his fingers. "Please Remember What's First – P, R, W, F. Protection. We're out of the sea and the currents. That was the big danger.

"Rescue – we'll need to build a signal fire to attract attention. That's the next priority because there's no point risking not being rescued because we're too busy looking after ourselves. Then water, because you die in a couple of days without it. And then food. Because, well, food. We can see if we can find more coconuts, for a start. Plus, the sea is nature's ultimate larder"

"There was food for several days in the cabin," Jian observed. And even though he was trying to drag Jian's thoughts away from the wreck, Beck glanced over to where the mast marked its position. Jian had a point. It would be difficult to reach, but it was there. Food in the cabin, and flares in the cockpit lockers – two potential resources that they would be mad to waste.

"First, let's check out this beach for other resources," he said. Ju-Long nodded and picked up the two life buoys.

"Your turn to carry the net, Beck!"

"Agreed," he said with a wry laugh. He picked up the soggy mass and slung it over his shoulder. Then he nodded at the two life buoys that she was carrying. "But you can leave one of those. I'll be needing it."

CHAPTER 9

B eck could easily have swum the distance back to *Dolphin* unaided, but he didn't. A survivor did not take unnecessary risks. If that meant using a little assistance, you swallowed your pride and you used it. And so he took one of the life buoys, letting it prop up the upper half of his body and feeling like a little kid learning to swim with a flotation aid in the public swimming pool. It also meant that if there was any hidden rip current that could potentially sweep him away then he would have more chance of using his strength to get back to the island.

This was a risk worth taking – but Beck knew he had to do this now. By now the tide was almost halfway back in again, and the more he waited, the more water there would be on top of the wreck. It wouldn't start going out again until after sunset. That would be the danger time also for any rip currents. He had made another sling out of the plastic netting, which was tied to the buoy and would carry whatever he retrieved from the sunken yacht.

It took just five minutes to reach the mast.

He tied the life buoy to one of the stays – the metal cables that ran from the tips of the crosstrees down to the deck – and then just let himself float, carried gently up and down by the half-metre swell of the sea. He gazed calmly at the horizon and put his mind into as relaxed a state as he could summon, letting go of all the thoughts, worries and excitements that had dominated the last couple of hours. He simply began to breathe, slowly, deeply, in and out, over and over again.

Ju-Long would have said he was preparing his *ki* energy. She had showed him a similar exercise when they were trekking through the jungle on their rescue mission. Beck just called it preparing his body for a deep dive. Either way, it was a kind of meditation, preparing him for what he had to do, and he had to get this right.

They had talked through the physics together.

"If there are ten metres of water on top of *Dolphin*," she had said, "then the pressure is the equivalent of an extra atmosphere. So, the air in your lungs will be squeezed to half its volume on the surface."

So, half the usual amount of air to work with, and he would be exerting himself, blind in the salt water, with his heart working overtime with adrenaline, in an extremely dangerous environment. He would need every atom of oxygen that his body could find.

Which meant, getting as much oxygen into his tissues as he could now, and flushing out as much carbon dioxide. The more his body burned up its oxygen, without replacing it with fresh breaths, the more carbon dioxide would build up, which was what triggered the desire to gulp in more air.

He held onto the life buoy and kept breathing steadily until he could feel his lungs stretching the inside of his chest.

Okay, almost ready to go, but he shouldn't just dive blind. He needed to know where he was going. Based on where the mast was, he pictured *Dolphin* lying on the sea bed. Bow would be to his left, stern to his right, which meant he could find the cockpit and the hatch into the cabin. He probably wouldn't be able to do this all in one dive, so the cockpit would be the first destination. There would be food on the island, even if he couldn't get the supplies up from the cabin, but the flares in the cockpit lockers were irreplaceable.

His body was buzzing with the extra oxygen he had taken in. There was no point delaying. He took a final breath, held it, and tipped himself headfirst down in the water. Hand over hand, he pulled himself below the surface, down the stay towards the boat.

It was like sliding into an alien world, a heartbeat away from the world he knew of air and light. Just a couple of metres below the surface, the water grew abruptly cold with a chill that began to eat into him. He kept his eyes shut against the sting of salt. The jagged refractions of light and dark would just confuse him anyway. Water pressed against him from all directions. A sharp pain in his ears told him that his ear drums were bowing under the pressure. He paused in his hand-over-hand progress to hold his nose tight and blew through it. Air pressure built up inside his head, forcing itself down the Eustachian tubes that ran between his throat and his inner ear, and pressing against his ear drums from the other direction, to counterbalance the water's weight. Squeaks and clicks and a distinct *pop* in each ear told him that the pressure had equalised. The pain vanished and he resumed his progress downwards.

Immersed in a medium where sound travels four times faster than in air, the depths were alive with strange whirs and whooshes. His body felt somehow both weightless, able to float off at a moment's notice, and strangely heavy – his lungs like a dead weight inside him, feeling heavier and heavier by the minute. Without the steel cable between his fingers he could have easily lost any sense of direction, to drift off into the dark with no idea which way was up, until all the oxygen was gone and he passed out. And if that happened, he knew he would be unconscious for about half a second before his body decided that that was it, game over, time to shut down for good. He fought that thought and pressed on.

His hands brushed against one of the ribbons that Jian had tied to the stay as a tell-tale for the wind direction. Good. That meant that in another metre he would be down to the guardrail. Then he could pull himself along to the cockpit –

Suddenly, a soft, billowing mass came out of nowhere and enveloped his arms and head, clinging onto him with a powerful grip. It was as if he had dived head first into the heart of a giant jellyfish that covered him up and would not let him go. He stopped abruptly and fought the panicked urge to breathe out his stored air in one gasp. His senses, already confused by the underwater scene, were now all firing off conflicting impulses so that he couldn't tell which way his body was facing or how to get free from the grasp of whatever it was. He felt more of it, gently settling onto him and holding him in a grip of cold, molten iron. Its suction and dead weight just wanted to draw him further down into the depths.

But he was still holding onto the stay. Heart pounding against his ribs, lungs feeling fit to burst, he made himself methodically reverse his course back up the metal cable, hand over hand in the other direction. The force that was gripping him didn't want him to go. He felt a harsh, rough surface scraping against his skin as he pulled himself free.

And then he was out of it. He risked opening his eyes, and even though they burned, immediately he could see the difference between the dark depths below and the sunlight above. He kicked his way up to the surface, following the training he remembered from his scuba course as a scout – clenching a fist above his head in case he came up underneath anything, and breathing out as he went so that the air in his lungs could safely expand as the pressure fell, without rupturing.

He broke the surface a few metres away from the mast and gulped for air.

Okay, scratch that plan.

He had already worked out what the problem was, and he knew there was no point trying again. It was the mainsail. It must have unfurled itself from the boom – they hadn't had time to tie it down properly – and it had draped itself across the rear half of the yacht. It was an impenetrable barrier, and going into that with anything less than proper scuba gear, like facemask and air tank, would be suicide.

It meant that everything on board *Dolphin* was off limits. The food, the flares – and hey, all those square metres of sailcloth themselves would have been mighty handy to a stranded group of survivors.

But that wasn't going to happen.

Beck swam over to where he had left the buoy, still bobbing next to the stay. He untied it and pushed himself back off towards the island.

"Plan B," he muttered.

CHAPTER 10

Beck stood at the island's highest point.

It had taken ten minutes to get up here from sea level, picking his way around fallen typhoon-damaged plant life. The centre of the island, out of reach of the tides, was completely covered in tightly packed undergrowth – a few palms, and the rest bushes and shrubs that he couldn't immediately identify.

The island wasn't big. He estimated he probably wasn't more than ten or twelve metres above the water, and even at low tide it couldn't be more than two hundred metres across. What Beck could see of its shape reminded him of an egg dropped into a pan to fry.

Ahead, and slightly lower than him, he could see the promontory that had stopped him earlier, when he had tried to get around the island. *Good,* he thought, *I know what I'll do with you.*

He turned a slow circle, gazing out to sea, getting his direction from the sun. It was coming up to four p.m., which meant that it was halfway between where it had been at noon – due south – and the western horizon where it would set. Knowing that, he could tell what was in which direction.

Most ways he looked, there was only sea, and then more sea beyond it. Northwards, where he knew the land was, there was a haze on the horizon and he couldn't see the mainland. He remembered from the chart that they were right at the far end of the archipelago. The only land nearby was ...

He turned to look north-east. Another island, about one kilometre away. He narrowed his eyes as he studied it. Without binoculars, he couldn't make out much detail. It looked larger than this one, maybe twice the size, also overgrown. It looked like the trees came further down towards the water. There was a light strip between blue sea and green leaves, which he guessed might be a beach. So, that island over there could be a friendlier place than this one.

But, this was the island they had at the moment, and one of the first rules of survival was to stay put, unless you have a very good reason for moving on. Rescuers are going to find it a lot easier to locate and rescue a stationary target. Plus of course, the only thing they had – at the moment – for crossing that stretch of water was a couple of life buoys.

No – unless this island proved uninhabitable, this was where they would stick it out.

When he had been exploring the shoreline, he had begun to build a map in his head of the island. Now he had seen enough of the island's layout to fill it in. That would help plan their future movements. He turned to head back down to the shore and join the others, and put out a hand to move a bush aside.

The bush rustled violently as something large moved inside it. Beck stepped quickly back, just as a reptilian head shot forward and snapped its teeth at where his leg had been.

"Whoah!"

Beck slowly crouched down and, from a safe distance, looked into the face of a Chinese dragon. And it was poised to bite.

CHAPTER 11

"Wow!" Beck murmured. He made no sudden movements, nothing to spook it – but he also tensed his legs to move very quickly indeed, if he had to.

He had seen pictures of these creatures but never met one in real life. He was looking at a Five-Fingered Golden Dragon. All he could see was the head – smooth and blunt, about thirty centimetres long, its scales a blend of yellow and dark gold. He knew that the rest of the body behind it, hidden in the bushes, could be up to two metres long, and it was studying him with cold, emotionless eyes, just as closely as he was studying it. And though those eyes were set in the sides of its head, they both faced forward – the true sign of a predator. Forward-facing eyes meant binocular vision and depth perception – vital for homing in accurately on prey.

A forked tongue flicked back and forth, in and out of its mouth. Snakes and lizards smell through their tongues, so the dragon was having a good sniff at him.

He quickly ran through in his head what he knew about the dragons. Unfortunately, it wasn't much. They were members of the monitor lizard family, which meant they had long, muscular bodies and necks, and powerful claws and tails. If it came to a race, the dragon could probably outrun him.

And he didn't know about Five-Fingered Golden Dragons specifically, but he did know about their cousins, Komodo

Dragons – another type of monitor lizard. It wasn't good. Komodos were active, aggressive hunters that would wait in long grass to ambush their prey. And they weren't worried about the size of whatever they were attacking, because their bite was fatal. It wasn't poisonous, like a snake – the dragon just had so many different types of deadly bacteria breeding in its mouth that its victim would simply die of the infection. The Komodo would take a nip, then just hang around waiting for you to fall over dead from toxic shock.

If the same went for this kind of dragon, then they were in trouble. Without moving his head, Beck looked left and right for anything he could use in defence if the dragon decided to have a go at him.

"So, this is your island, I guess?" he mumbled. It hissed at him again, and slowly withdrew its head. Neither of them took their eyes off the other until it was out of sight.

Beck breathed out and made his way back to the shore, taking extra care with his route and keeping an eye out for any other potential dragons hiding out.

So, they were sharing limited space on an island with at least one two-metre long carnivore with a poisonous bite. And almost definitely more. This was not a situation he would have chosen.

CHAPTER 12

"**D**ragons?" Jian exclaimed. It was the most interest he had shown in anything since he was injured.

They had rendezvoused back at the beach that Ju-Long had found. The sea had swept up a long ramp of gravel through a break in the rocks, all the way up to the base of the high ground. It was on the eastern side of the island, with a view of the other island that Beck had seen.

It wasn't perfect – if it had been larger, and sandy, Beck would have marked out the word "SOS" in large letters, to attract the attention of any low flying aircraft. It was the international distress signal, even in Chinese, Beck smiled to himself. But the area was too small for that – thin, and narrow, and not sandy. Still, it would be a good place to camp. The top of the beach was surrounded by rocks and the cliff, and it was overhung slightly by trees, so it was shaded. The sun was beating down hard on the rest of the island, but here they were a comfortable temperature and not at risk of burning. The end of the beach was cut off by a natural staircase of boulders, piled up one on top of the other, with another of those dark stains that showed water was running very slowly down it.

There was a plus to it not being sandy, and that was the absence of sandflies – tiny, buzzy little blood suckers that could end up covering you in a red rash of bites. If they had been around, Beck would have considered building a camp in the middle of the island, as far from the sand as they could get.

But there were no sandflies, plus the cool shore winds down here would keep the mozzies away. They could camp a few comfortable metres beyond the high water mark, so the waves wouldn't reach them, and they would be safe. They hoped.

At the moment, it was dragon-free, but Beck had no idea how long that would last.

"Do you know how many?" Ju-Long asked.

"There can't be many on an island this size," Beck said. "More than one, obviously, because they've got to breed. Maybe a small family of them. Any more than that, and they'd eat up all their resources. And probably each other."

"Resources, yes," Ju-Long said. "They must have food. If they can eat it, so can we."

"They probably swim and catch fish. Or crabs. Or birds," Jian suggested.

"What I want to know is, can we live on the same island as them safely?" Beck asked. "If they're used to having to fight for food, and they decide it would be easier to take a bite at us ..."

Jian and Ju-Long looked at each other.

"What I want to know," Jian said, "is, can we eat them?"

"What?" Ju-Long and Beck said together, as though he had just said something really odd. Jian looked from one to the other in surprise.

"Well?"

"The one thing I do know about them," said Beck, "is they're endangered. In China, anyway. They're on the China Species Red List."

"And Beck won't kill an endangered animal," Ju-Long explained, in response to Jian's baffled look. "When we were in the gorge, he wouldn't even kill a turtle for that reason."

"We won't need to kill them – we're smarter than that," Beck said. "If they can eat fish and crabs, so can we," he added to reassure him. "So, did you find any sources of water?"

While he explored the interior of the island, Ju-Long had been finishing off her exploration of the edges.

"Just more like this." She pointed at the dark marks on the cliff at the top of the beach. "And these." She held up two full, unopened bottles of a fizzy soft drink. Beck's eyebrows went up.

"Okay. These will do nicely."

Jian's face lit up as Beck took the bottles and began to unscrew the lids. Then he almost shouted, "no!" as Beck held them upside down and their contents gurgled out to the ground. The drink fizzed and bubbled as it disappeared into the gravel. He stared at the stain on the pebbles.

"Why did you do that?"

Beck grinned.

"Trust me, this is all chemical and it would only make you thirsty again. The whole point of companies selling fizzy drinks is to make you want to buy more fizzy drinks. Whereas..."

With these and the bottle he had found earlier, they now had three – one each. He gathered them all up and headed to the top of the beach.

The dark stain of water dribbled over a small ridge in the cliff face, and then fell half a metre to the beach. There wasn't enough to make a decent stream that would flow down the beach – it all just disappeared into the gravel – but it was perfect for what he wanted. He pushed each of the three bottles into the gravel, base first, to hold them up. Then, one by one, he cut three lengths of rope from the net that were a bit longer than the distance from the ridge to the mouths of the bottles.

He laid the three lengths side by side on the ridge, holding them in place with small stones. The lengths each dangled down into a bottle, and he made sure that the ropes went well into the bottle mouth.

Jian and Ju-Long had followed him, out of curiosity. They peered closely at his handiwork, and then Jian laughed. It was the first sign of happiness he had shown since *Dolphin* went down and it was nice to hear.

"Oh, very good!" he said.

The water that trickled down the rock face was now trickling down the rope instead. Surface tension made it cling to the fibres and gravity kept it heading downhill. And so, it slid down the rope, drop by drop, and into the bottles. It would be their own personal water bank.

"These are half litre bottles," Beck estimated. The labels were long gone but he recognised the size. "So, in about an hour we'll each have half a litre to drink. Over six hours, we'll each get our three litres of water a day. Now, let's see what else we've got ..."

***

By the time the first hour was up, and the bottles were full, Ju-Long and Beck had scoured the island, plundering the treasures they had found on their first venture. Jian, to his frustration, had to sit and wait. He tried to come with them, at first, but then he stumbled and went white as even that small bump jarred his arm. After that he agreed, fuming, that it would be best to sit and wait quietly.

They went in different directions and had to make a couple of journeys to bring back everything they found – thanks to the typhoon, so much had been washed into the sea and was still swirling around, waiting to be washed up wherever there was a shoreline. Jian happily made himself useful by sorting it all into two piles.

The first pile was just bits of wood. There was a lot of it, ranging from small branches to a large chunk of a fishing boat that had probably been wrecked and smashed up by the typhoon. It consisted of a long, flat section of planks nailed together, which must have been almost a quarter of the hull. It would never be a boat again but it would be a handy source of material, and not just for burning. Beck could already think of a couple of other uses.

The other pile was all kinds of assorted garbage. The typhoon must have ripped most of it off the mainland and the sea currents had brought it here. Among the items that Beck could immediately think of a use for...

Five more flip-flops, of different shapes and sizes. They were all made of bubble-filled foam, so had floated easily. There was not one pair among them, which made Beck wonder if there were a lot of one-footed Chinese on holiday somewhere.

A metal saucepan. Jian had seen a small metal tube sticking out of the gravel of the beach and pulled on it – it turned out to be the handle. It was full of soaking wet grit, but that was easy to rinse away.

A sheet of tough, clear plastic, clouded by scratches.

And several more plastic bottles, which Beck set up to fill alongside the ones already in the water bank.

Beck studied the piles of debris as he sipped from one of the full bottles and savoured the feel of clean, cool water refreshing his system.

"Funny, isn't it," he said thoughtfully. "One man's trash is another man's treasure. To us, these could all be life or death. But their original owners probably won't even miss them." He paused. "Except maybe the five people who don't have a matching flip-flop."

They all chuckled.

"So, how will the flip-flops be useful to us?" Ju-Long asked, not quite believing.

Beck grinned. "Oh, I can think of a way..."

CHAPTER 13

Beck stepped back and admired his handiwork. A wooden tripod stood on top of the rocky promontory on the edge of the island.

"Pretty good," he murmured, "and we can keep adding to it, as well."

This was the second element of Protection, Water, Rescue and Food. They would never be rescued if no one saw them here. The promontory would be their signal point. Up here they could light a fire, a beacon – not for light or warmth, just to be seen.

Beck had picked all the bits of wood he wanted from the pile on the beach. It had taken him several trips to get everything up here – the signal point and the beach were almost on opposite sides of the island – and everywhere he went, he kept himself braced to fight off any hungry dragons. But this was where the signal fire had to be. It was high up, on the edge of the island where there would be nothing to obscure it. And it was more likely that vessels would pass by on this side, where there was nothing but open water, than try to sail between the islands.

The tripod was a little taller than he was. He had lashed two planks together at one end, first tying a simple hitch knot around both of them, then wrapping the rope several times over the knot, top to bottom and left to right. Then he had wedged the third plank into the groove between the first two at the top, and tied that one in place as well.

He had stood the tripod up, and built a small platform about half way up. First he had tied three slightly shorter pieces of wood, each one across two of the legs like horizontal struts to make a triangle. Then he could lay more wood across these to build the platform itself.

But a fire, of course, needed stuff to burn. He had a collection of dry sticks that he had gathered up from the undergrowth behind him, and with his knife, he whittled the bark away into dry shavings that would act as the tinder – the bit that he actually set fire to. He piled it up into a light, fluffy heap on the platform. Air could circulate freely all around it, and once he applied flame, it would lick its way through the mass in seconds.

On top of that, he laid the kindling – the sticks that he had shaved down. They would catch fire off the tinder and give energy to burn the fuel. At least, that was the theory.

If this was a camp fire, or a cooking fire, the fuel would be a couple of logs, or at least larger pieces of wood. They would burn slowly, but surely, releasing their heat over hours.

But instead of wood fuel, Beck carefully laid the flip-flops on top of the platform. He didn't want heat, he wanted smoke – lots of it. The artificial foam would give off thick, black clouds of the stuff – choking and foul, but very visible. Grey or white smoke could easily get lost in the sea haze, and anyone on a passing boat could simply miss it. But there was something about black smoke that immediately told a watcher this wasn't natural. The eye wouldn't just filter it out. It would be about as visible as it could be.

Beck squatted down on his haunches and fingered the two halves of the fire steel that hung around his neck – the other personal item that he carried with him everywhere, together with his knife. It could light a fire almost anywhere. He gazed out to sea, and thought.

Jian had suggested trying to keep the fire burning, 24/7. It might increase the chances of being spotted, he had pointed out.

But they would have to be constantly replenishing it, Beck had replied, which would be so time consuming, taking up energy that could be better used in looking after themselves. The tripod itself would burn through eventually and need replacing. And those flip-flops would only burn once.

So, they had all agreed that the better option was to leave it until it was absolutely needed – when there was a boat sailing near, or an aircraft flying low. If they spotted either of those then they could run to the signal fire and have it blazing in minutes. Then at night they would keep their normal fire burning, right where they would sleep.

So, the last step for this signal fire was to protect the beacon against the weather. If it rained, the fire pile would soak through. He had passed a palm tree on the way up here, so he headed back to it and cut off an armful of fronds, as long as his forearm and about half as wide. He went back to the beacon and laid them around the pile on the platform, overlapping, so that any rain which fell on them couldn't find a way in. The leaves were natural gutters, each folded lengthways into a V-shape, and rain would be channelled down them.

Last of all, he tied a couple of strands of net rope around them to hold them in place.

"Sorted," he murmured. Now it was time to go down and see how the others were doing at the job he had left them with, and work out a watch rota. Beck noticed how thirsty he was – he had finished off the bottle he had brought with him. But he knew the other bottles in the water bank should have topped up by now.

He picked up his shirt and dusted himself down with it, before pulling it back on. It had been hot work, so he had taken it off and rubbed earth over the top half of his body. The point had no trees to provide shade, and the sun still beat down on it, even though by now it was getting on for five p.m. – two hours to sunset – and the earth made a crude but effective sunblock.

The factor was somewhere between fifteen and yuk, but all you needed was an extra millimetre of something to take the force of the sun before it hit your skin.

He turned to go, but froze like a statue where he stood. Beck found himself staring in terror at two of the dragons, side by side, cutting off his way from the point.

CHAPTER 14

"So, most definitely not alone," he said softly.

They didn't look pleased to see him, and it was mutual. Their front legs were braced and their heads were raised up. Beck tried to figure out if it was the way they just liked to stand, or if they were about to charge. It was the first time he had got a clear look at one, since the first had been mostly hidden in the bushes. The smallest was about as long as he was tall. Its body seemed to be slung between its legs so that it was hanging from its thigh and shoulder joints, rather than balanced on top of them, like a mammal would be, but the legs themselves were powerful and muscular, and long claws dug into the dirt.

One of them hissed. It didn't keep coming, but it didn't take a step back either.

Reptiles didn't have expressions. Beck had found this before. Snakes, crocodiles – you couldn't tell what they were thinking by looking. So, he had no idea if these ones fancied a feast of fourteen year old boy, or were afraid of him, or were maybe just annoyed that he had taken their space...

He looked again at the point, and tried to picture it through lizard eyes. Lizards were cold blooded, and they got their energy by sunning themselves. They would choose somewhere nice and exposed, preferably rocky so it would absorb the sun's warmth.

Somewhere like the point. Well, duh. He had nicked their lounging spot.

"Okay, so I kind of barged in, didn't I?" he muttered quietly. "Well, it's big enough for all of us. I won't bother you if you don't bother me. Deal?"

The other lizard hissed, and they both flicked their tongues at him. Beck hoped they weren't smelling him to decide if he was edible.

Beck slowly bent down and picked up one of the spare pieces of wood. He gripped it at one end in both hands, poised, ready to defend himself if he had to.

"I'll be off now." Beck spoke softly and calmly. "Lovely to have had this chat. But I'm going to have to come back. We need to keep watch for rescue from up here during the day. Just warning you both."

Slowly, always keeping himself turned towards them, he sidled his way off the point. It brought him to within a couple of metres of the pair. They didn't move, didn't even turn their heads to follow him, but he had a feeling their eyes swivelled in their sockets, tracking him all the way.

Okay, whoever was on watch would need to make sure they protected themselves, from dragons and from the heat of the sun.

He set off back to the beach, keeping the stick at the ready all the way. Now he knew there were at least two dragons on this island; there could be more.

Their situation was getting worse by the hour.

CHAPTER 15

"**D**o you remember what I said about the Chinese space station?" Ju-Long asked. It took Beck a moment to remember, but then he laughed.

"Oh, yes. Of course."

They were back at the beach, gazing at the results of Ju-Long and Jian's handiwork. This was where they would be spending their nights.

The undergrowth that covered the island came down to the top of the beach, and a tree right on the edge had stuck a pair of thick branches out across the gravel, side by side and almost horizontal, about a metre off the ground. With Jian passing her things one-handedly, Ju-Long had used the section of the fishing boat and other bits of wood to build a platform, laid across the two branches and tied in place with more lengths from the rope net.

Then she had taken the four longest poles they could find and jammed them into the beach, so that they stuck up above the platform, one at each corner. She had tied crosspieces to the tops of each one, using the same sort of diagonal lashing that Beck had used on the beacon, so that there was a square frame above the platform. Then she had tied the last few of the long pieces of wood at spaces across the frame to make rafters.

Meanwhile Jian had cut palm fronds which she could lay over the rafters, overlapping, like Beck's protective layer on the beacon, but on a larger scale. Jian had also arranged more fronds on the platform itself, as a very basic kind of futon to make sleeping there slightly more comfortable, and he had arranged some cut-off branches along the seaward side of the platform to make a primitive windbreak.

They would only spend time on the platform when they slept, so they would be lying down. The windbreak would keep the breeze from the sea off their bodies. It might only make a difference of a degree or so, but even in these subtropical seas, that difference could be vital. Beck had suggested one other way to keep warm up on the platform: to build a fire on the gravel, directly beneath their camp. The other two had looked at each other, concerned, but Beck had reassured them that it would work.

Beck suspected that all this exercise had taken more out of Jian than he was prepared to admit. He was definitely cradling his hurt arm, though it was still supported by its sling, and his skin had an unhealthy pallor to it.

"Yup," Beck agreed with a straight face, "that is definitely the next best thing to a space station. If it was at a slightly higher orbit – like, several hundred kilometres above the earth – then I don't think I could tell them apart."

Jian was looking baffled.

"Space station?"

"When we were going down the river gorge," Ju-Long explained, "Beck and I built a raft from bamboo poles. I felt as proud of that as I do that China has built a space station."

"Tiangong-1," Jian agreed with a proud nod. "I see." He held his good arm out. "Well, if your raft was Tiangong-2, welcome to Tiangong-3!" he announced. His smile seemed force but Beck was sure the intent was genuine, and he was glad. Jian would continually have to pull himself up to being his old self, and Beck admired his positivity and courage.

"Congratulations on being the first Young Pioneers in space," Beck laughed. "Let's celebrate with a drink."

He picked three of the bottles from the water bank and carefully removed the dangling lengths of rope before handing them out one at a time, to Ju-Long and Jian. He took the last one himself and raised it in a toast, with a wry smile.

"To China."

He put the bottle to his lips. Even though his body wanted him to tilt it back and glug it all down in one go, he went more slowly. He let a little into his mouth and swilled it around, feeling it coat his tongue and the back of his throat. Then he gargled a little, and moistened his lips. And only then did he swallow it. His eyes closed, savouring the feeling.

"Like gold, isn't it?" The other two nodded, then raised their bottles and together they drank.

As Beck slowly drained his bottle his thoughts were moving on to the next job. Protection, rescue, water – they had now ticked three of the four essentials off the to-do-list. The fourth was easier done in the daylight. He checked his watch, even though he could already see the sun heading for the horizon. They only had about an hour of daylight left.

Ju-Long took the bottles back to their filling station at the foot of the cliff and re-inserted the dripping rope strands.

Meanwhile, Beck was picking his way through the unused pieces of wood. There was a carved round piece about the width of a broom handle – straight and about as long as his arm. He hefted it in his hand experimentally. It had a good weight to it – not too heavy, but strong enough to carry the force of any thrust that he made. It wouldn't bend too much under force.

"Okay." he said. He looked first at Ju-Long, then at Jian. Jian so badly wanted to be doing something useful – something that he could safely do with one hand and which wouldn't wear him out. "Jian, how do you fancy taking the first shift at the signal beacon?"

Jian smiled happily by way of answer. It was something useful that he could do without pain.

"And Ju-Long – we're going to need some sort of a shelter up there, so we don't get burnt up by the sun. Maybe not this evening, but certainly tomorrow."

"We can make one," she said diplomatically, and Jian lowered his eyes. They all knew it would be more accurate to say that she could build one, with Jian's assistance. She picked through the wood and held up a couple of pieces. "These as supports, and some of the net as a roof, covered with leaves."

"Perfect. Look out for the dragons – take a good stick with you. And then, we'll need a fire to cook our dinner, back here at camp."

"But we don't yet have any dinner to cook," she pointed out.

"Nope." Beck grinned and hefted the piece of wood. "That's my job."

Protection, rescue, water ... and food.

CHAPTER 16

The gully in the rocks was as long and as wide as *Dolphin* had been, and waves surged in and out. Ju-Long had discovered the natural inlet on her exploration of the shoreline, and showed it to Beck. At low tide it would be dry but now, at nearly high tide, it was all covered in seawater. Fronds of seaweed beneath the surface swayed back and forth with the swell. Fish were silhouetted against the pale gravel as they glided to and fro with casual flicks of their tails, and crabs crawled slowly from crevice to crevice, just below the waterline.

Beck lay on the rocks and held his hand directly above one, so that even if it sensed his presence, it wouldn't be able to bring its claws up to bear on him. Then he grabbed swiftly down and snatched it out of the water.

He held it from behind, so that its claws and legs could wave helplessly but not hurt him, and then he quickly put it out of its misery, cracking the shell and levering the top half off with his knife. Ju-Long could do this much better than he could – as he had discovered in their previous adventure, when her Tai Chi crab-cracking skills had amazed him – but she already had enough to do.

The bottom half of the shell contained a glistening mix of firm, white crab meat and the sticky, wobbly pile that was its guts. He took a pinch of the guts between thumb and forefinger and flung it into the water at the top end of the inlet. Then another pinch, a short distance away.

"Here, fishy, fishy..." he murmured.

If the three of them had just wanted to exist on crab meat, they could probably do that. But they wouldn't get much energy from crabs this small. That's why Beck had bigger game in mind. Fish – and not just the little tiddlers that he could see down there. Fish had a good sense of smell and would be able to sniff this out from a couple of hundred metres away. *Yum, free crab guts,* they would think. And when they came...

He had pulled off his top and kicked off his trousers, to stand in just his shorts. Now he picked up his spear and gave it a final check.

The shaft was the straight piece of wood he had found earlier. He had sharpened one end into a point, but that wasn't all. He had retraced his steps after they had all come ashore, to find the dead bird. Even back then he had thought it might come in useful – now he knew how.

He had twisted the head off the neck so that he just had the skull and the beak. The two halves of the beak were strong and pointed – when it was alive, the bird would have dived head first into the water at high speed, and the beak was designed to take that force and to grab the fish the bird was aiming at.

Which was why Beck had firmly fastened it to the end of the spear with a whip knot, tugged tight. The spear now had three prongs – the two halves of the beak and the sharpened wooden end. Triple the reach and triple the killing power.

And now he just had to wait...

But not for long. The first sign was when the small shoals of tiddlers flicked their tails and discreetly vanished. Something large was moving up the inlet.

Beck picked up the spear as the fish came into view. From up here, distorted by refraction in the water, he couldn't make out exactly what it was. But it was a good half a metre long, and that was all he needed to know.

He took the spear in both hands and aimed it carefully down at the water, a little below where he could see the fish. The human eye always assumed light travelled in straight lines, but in fact the light would bend when it came out of the water and into the air, so the fish's position would be a little bit in front of where it seemed to be.

And, the fish was moving, which added to the challenge. Beck had to make his best estimate as to where it was now, and where it would be in a second's time.

He could see how deep the gully was and so he knew he wouldn't be jumping head first onto rocks. There was no time to hesitate.

He braced himself, and dived.

CHAPTER 17

The triple-pointed spear end was the first thing into the water, followed a fraction of a second later by Beck himself. He was using the same trick as the beak's original owner, diving head first, legs up, aligning all his weight and momentum with the spear to drive it down.

Water roared in his ears and salt water bit into his eyes. All he could see was confused shades of light and dark, with no way of telling what was a rock, a fish or anything else. He had to trust to the accuracy of his dive and that was all.

He felt a shudder through the shaft of the spear as it hit something and he thrust further down, intending to impale it or pin it against the bottom of the inlet before it could wiggle free. It grated against the bottom of the inlet. Well, he either had the fish or he didn't – there would be no second chances at this stage. He kicked upwards, back to the surface, blowing a cloud of bubbles as he went.

His head broke the surface and he lifted the spear out to check – but he could already feel it was too light. He pulled a face as he lifted it up to check. Sure enough, the three prongs were completely bare.

"Oh, well," he said with a grin. He fingered the rope that fastened the beak to the shaft. "At least the knot held and the prongs aren't broken!"

It was a basic lesson for any kind of hunting or surviving. Just do something once and you probably won't get anything.

You need patience, you need persistence, and you need to stay positive and hopeful.

He chucked the spear up onto the rocks and levered himself out of the water.

It took two more tries and more crab guts, but the patience was worth it.

On the second try he felt the spear hit the fish, and he felt the fish fighting back. The spear shook as it wriggled, and when he came up to the surface, the fish was gone. There was a small red cloud in the water, which meant he had gashed it, which he regretted because while he wanted to kill the fish for food, he didn't want to cause it unnecessary pain along the way. Very probably another fish would now take it, and make a better job of it than he had.

But hopefully the blood in the water would attract more like it into the inlet. The crab guts could only go so far.

The third time, he had the hang of it. You catch a fish on the end of your spear and the fish tries to swim away from it, so the secret was to keep the spear moving at all times. Keep pressing down, or up, but keep pressing *forwards*. Don't pull the spear back. If the fish tries to get away, just make sure the spear is following it. Don't give it a chance.

He needed both hands to guide the spear as the fish thrashed at the end. It was strong and powerful and heavy. Beck ground the spear against the rocky bottom and held it there, even though he could feel his lungs pressing against his ribs, until he felt the fish grow weaker. Then he quickly twisted around in the water, still keeping the spear moving, giving the fish no time to slip away.

He broke the surface with a whoop and hurled the spear onto the rocks, clambering quickly out after it all in one movement. The fish lay, impaled, flapping, gills gasping for breath, until he hit it firmly on the head with the handle of his knife.

It was a triggerfish – a body shaped like a flattened oval, a lot taller than it was wide, and fins on the rear half of its body, just in front of a small but powerful tail. Its mouth was also small, but Beck knew it could have delivered a powerful nip if it had got free.

And it was a good size – almost the size of his upper torso. Plenty for three hungry teenagers to eat.

He shook as much water off his body as he could, then pulled his dry clothes on and slid his fingers into the fish's gills to carry it back to the camp.

The sun was right on the horizon, and the sky to the west of the island was a glowing shade of pink. On the eastern side of the island, where the camp was, there was no sun at all now. Every colour around the beach was turning a shade of grey.

Ju-Long and Jian were back from the signal point, their duty done for the day. Ju-Long had also built a good fire on the beach, ready for the spark that would light it. Beck silently held his hand out to Jian. His fire steel usually lived on a chain around his neck, but he had loaned it to Jian while the other boy stood signal duty. Now Jian tugged it from around his neck with his good hand and passed it back to its owner.

The fire steel consisted of a rod of a substance called ferrocerium, and a flat metal plate. You hit the rod with the scraper plate, and sparks flew off it. It could light a fire just about everywhere except underwater.

Beck knelt down to prepare to strike sparks into the fire. Ju-Long had built it in much the same way as he had built the fire on the signal platform. A mass of tinder: dried leaves, weeds and twigs. Kindling: a small pyramid of larger twigs and sticks. And fuel: not flip-flops but washed up pieces of wood. It had been days since the last rain and everything had been dried out by sea breeze and sunshine.

Then Beck changed his mind.

"Jian, come and light for us, buddy."

Jian looked at Beck nervously.

"You sure? I haven't used one of these fire steels before."

"Good time to practice, then," Beck replied. He wanted Jian to feel both valued and needed, and Beck also knew that nothing built pride and confidence like lighting your own fire from scratch.

Jian leapt to the task and, with Beck holding the rod and Jian the striker in his one good hand, together they started to strike sparks. The fire caught in seconds. Yellow light began to flicker inside and the wood began to crackle and snap, as air and steam trapped inside its fibres expanded and burst out into the open.

Jian smiled at Beck. "Awesome!" he added, as he returned the fire steel to Beck.

Ju-Long and Jian sat on logs and huddled around it, letting the warmth soak into their bones. Beck laid the triggerfish down on a rock and deftly sliced it open down its belly from mouth to tail, taking care not to puncture the guts. He stuck a finger into the gash and hooked it around the inedible mass of stomach and intestines, then pulled them all out in a sharp tug and dropped them into the pit he had dug out of the gravel for the purpose. Without the dragons around, he would have just chucked everything far away into the bushes, but he didn't want to attract carnivorous visitors to the beach. Now he could safely cut the fish open and carve off slices of glistening, white meat.

"Here." Beck passed each of them one of the fish's eyeballs. "Plenty of fluid and highly nutritious." He smiled irrepressibly.

Jian took his without a fuss. Ju-Long politely declined hers, with a wry grin.

"Two eyes, three of us – and the one who caught it surely deserves the prize."

"Ha! If you insist. Thanks." Beck popped it into his mouth and felt it burst into thick, salty liquid as he bit down. He grimaced. Okay, it was nutritious, but not the tastiest meal. He kept chewing – which took a while – until he felt able to swallow it, and washed it down with a chug from his bottle.

After that, they impaled the slices of fish on sticks and held them out to the fire, letting the heat from the flames do the magical work of turning raw flesh into food. There would be plenty here for second helpings, too. They sat happily in the fire's circle of warmth and light, driving back the subtropical night that had fallen quickly over the island. The temperature had only dropped three or four degrees, Beck estimated – enough for them to notice, not so low as to be a problem.

The stars had emerged as the blue of the sky faded to dark. There were no clouds to obscure the million little diamond pinpricks scattered above them, in layers that were light years deep, but it always amazed Beck how so many sources of light up there could still produce so little light down here on the ground.

Deprived of sunlight, the sea no longer sparkled blue. It was black and mysterious, unknowable. A sliver of moon cast a silver sheen on the horizon but, nearby, only the gently breaking waves showed any sign of life as they caught the flickering light from the fire.

Jian suddenly drew a breath, staring at the ground. It was obviously the prelude to saying something that still went unspoken. They looked at him and waited.

"Today..." Jian began eventually. He pulled a face. "Today has not gone exactly as planned. But, thank you, Beck. And Ju-Long. For all your help."

"Nothing was your fault, Jian," Ju-Long assured him. He pulled another face, more sceptical. Beck was sure he didn't agree with her. He still blamed himself for losing *Dolphin*.

"Well, we have each other," Beck said. "Someone once told me that a survivor needs the three Fs to get along. Family, faith and food. Okay, we're not technically family, but it feels like it. Or even friends instead. It's still an F."

"I have faith," Ju-Long said. "Faith in us and faith that we will survive. I know what skills we all have. We are all healthy and we have brains. We can take charge of our situation."

"And the food is smelling good." Jian waved his stick, and sniffed. "Maybe another minute."

"And out here I would rather have my friends – you two – than my family, to be honest," Ju-Long said with a laugh. "My parents are wonderful – but they would be panicking like crazy right now!"

"I think my father could cope," Jian said, and Beck remembered the capable Mr Zhou, who had held the expedition together while they were stranded on the ledge.

"And, Beck," Ju-Long said, "I know your parents are dead and you live with your uncle. What about any brothers or sisters – do you have any?"

"No," he confirmed with a sad face. And then: "Well – not anymore."

They looked at him in surprise – almost as much surprise as he was feeling. Why had he suddenly started thinking about this? He almost never did. He had always known about it – his parents hadn't been the kind to hide stuff from him – but he couldn't remember the last time he had mentioned it to anyone except Uncle Al. If at all.

"I was one of twins," he explained, to answer the question on their faces. "I had a baby sister born at the same time. Only, she died. I only know about her because my parents told me. They had time to name her Dian Rachel Granger, after Dian Fossey and Rachel Carson, who were two women my mother really admired. But then she got ill. She only lived for a day."

He gazed without any focus into the fire. Somewhere at home, he knew, there was a photo album – a very slim photo album – containing the only evidence Dian had ever existed. Maybe he would look it up when he got back home.

"Of course, I don't remember her at all. So, yeah, basically I've always been an only child –"

But he had no more time to talk about it, because a sudden weight slammed into his back and knocked him from his seat, head first into the fire. He twisted in mid-air to avoid the flames and landed sprawled in the sand. His stick and his slice of fish went flying.

Jian and Ju-Long scrambled to their feet, and Jian dropped straight back onto his knees again with a shout of pain, clutching his injured wrist as the sudden movement jarred his bones.

From a distance of only a few inches, Beck found himself looking into the gleaming eyes and gaping jaws of a dragon.

Then the dragon lunged.

CHAPTER 18

Beck flung himself out of the way, arms and legs scrambling, so that when he hit the ground he immediately launched himself even further out of biting range.

But it wasn't him that the dragon was aiming for. Its jaws seized on the dropped lump of cooked fish. Then it scuttled forward and gulped up the bits of fish that Jian and Ju-Long had dropped onto the sand. It downed them in one swallow while Beck stared at it in disbelief.

"Back right away, guys, and keep your eyes on him."

The dragon hissed at them and snapped its powerful jaws. Beck was closest to it, and the two of them stood, locked in a mutual stand-off. Without moving his head, Beck tried to locate anything he could use as a weapon.

"Look!" Ju-Long called.

Another dragon emerged from the dark, just long enough to snatch the rest of the fish off the rock where Beck had left it.

Then both dragons turned and wandered off into the darkness.

Beck kicked sand after them.

"Wow, those dudes don't mess about. And that was our dinner." But then he noticed something much more important. Ju-Long was helping Jian to his feet. The older boy clutched his injured arm to his chest and his face was frozen with suppressed pain.

"Jian, are you all right?"

"I think so." Jian straightened up slowly, but kept holding his hand. "I moved too quickly for my bones to catch up. They are complaining very loudly but they are getting quieter."

"Were those the same two you saw earlier?" Ju-Long asked.

"I think so, or at least, I hope so," Beck said. He still felt adrenaline pumping. And he still felt angry. It was the time and the effort gone into catching that fish, just to give two dragons a meal they hadn't worked for at all – and it was the fact that he himself hadn't thought of keeping a proper watch. He had already known they were on the island. He should have been more aware.

Ju-Long picked up the stick she had used to hold the fish to the fire.

"I was looking forward to that," she said sadly. "I suppose we can go hungry for a night."

"No flipping way are we going hungry," Beck vowed. He glared out into the darkness, in the direction the dragons had taken. No, he was not going to give those wretched creatures the satisfaction.

"Are you going to go diving again? In the dark?" Jian asked. Beck shook his head and looked out to sea.

"Not quite. I won't be diving, and it won't be dark."

***

The tripod stood in half a metre of water, just off the shore. It was almost identical to the signal beacon – perhaps a little smaller. Beck had raided the pile of driftwood to build it – three legs, and a platform halfway up its height where a small fire now blazed.

Conditions were just right. Its feet were weighed down with rocks to stop it rocking in the gentle swell. Beck had covered the platform with a layer of sand to stop it burning through, and the light lit up a circle of sea all around it. A few metres away the water was black, but it slowly glimmered into life the closer it got to the platform. This close, it was almost transparent.

Ju-Long and Jian waited on the shore a few metres away. Beck stood in his shorts with the water just lapping up to his thighs. He could see his bare feet, and he could see the water grow hazier as plankton came in – small clouds of microscopic creatures drifting mindlessly, attracted by the light. And where the plankton went, fish followed.

He stood stock still while he took his pick of the prey, letting the fish think he was some kind of rock. There were the usual tiddlers, sticking together for security. A crab sidled around the edge of the light, maybe not wanting to get too close. *Sensible crab*, Beck thought.

And then the first likely candidate for dinner came casually swimming into view. It nosed at the legs of the tripod and drifted away with a flick of its fins. Beck stayed exactly where he was. It had to come in front of him. Any motion by him now would just scare it off.

The fish was in no hurry. The smaller fish had disappeared and it was obviously confident in its size.

Beck slowly lifted the spear, ready for the thrust.

"Come on, my beauty," Beck murmured. "There we go!" He brought the spear down with lightning speed.

"Bingo!" he shouted as he heaved the fish onto the beach.

This time only Jian cooked the fish, while Beck and Ju-Long faced the other way, backs to the fire, wooden clubs in their hands, eyes peeled for dragons. None came. They continued to keep watch while they ate their portions, bit by bit. The dragons were obviously satisfied for the time being.

"What worries me," Beck said quietly, "is them learning to associate us with food. Then they'll never let us alone."

"They are big enough to get onto the platform," Ju-Long said.

"Yup. So we don't give them any reason to. Eat up."

There was no point staying awake after their delayed meal. It had been a long, long day. Even though they all felt keyed up with nervous energy, Beck knew it would vanish pretty well the moment they lay down and let themselves relax.

But, thanks to the dragons, there were a couple more things to do.

First, he and Ju-Long arranged an anti-dragon device on each side of the platform. At each end of each side, they put down a bit of driftwood, sticking over the edge and weighed down at the platform end with a rock. Beck balanced longer bits of wood across the other ends of each pair. Any dragon that tried to climb onto the platform would put its weight on one of the long bits of wood. It would weigh more than the stones holding it up, and flip the anti-dragon device off the platform. The noise would wake them up, and hopefully the surprise would be enough to deter the dragon from getting any closer without the humans having to take any further defensive measures. It was simple and ingenious.

And just in case that wasn't enough, they hung the net from the roof supports, around all four sides of the platform. They would sleep inside its protection. *The world's worst mosquito net,* Beck thought.

Just before climbing onto their platform they piled up several large bits of driftwood onto the fire. Some of the heat and smoke would drift over them during the night, helping deter mosquitoes, keep the three survivors warm, and hopefully keep the dragons away. Fire has always been mankind's greatest weapon and also the most potent way of stopping predators from entering your domain.

They clambered onto the platform to sleep. Jian with his one good hand could only prop his backside on the edge and then lever himself up. They arranged themselves top-to-tail on the layer of palm fronds, with Jian in the middle, lying on his back, all of them huddled together to share warmth. Jian and Ju-Long used the life buoys as pillows. Beck used the block of polystyrene.

He lay on his side, eyes open, thinking about the day past and planning for the one to come. First thing in the morning, he would –

No, stop that, he told himself. *You already know what to do. You don't need to be thinking about it now. Sleeping is more important…*

And sure enough, he felt the drowsiness steal up on him and his eyes grow heavy.

He could tell from the sound of Jian's breathing, and the impatient shifting of his body, that the older boy was nowhere near falling asleep. Uncomfortable, and probably in more pain than he would admit to. There wasn't much Beck could do about that.

"The fire should last until morning – well, at least the embers. But toss a log on if either of you wake up in the night, eh?"

And with that, Beck fell asleep.

Beck felt someone tap him awake. He opened his eyes to see a smiling girl with dark hair like his, shoulder length. She sat on the edge of the platform and gave him a playful prod.

"Dian?" Beck found he was staring at her, but she didn't seem to mind. "Is that you? I always wondered what you'd look like."

"You can't have always wondered. You haven't thought about me for ages, until tonight."

She stood up and wandered around the edge of the platform, peering into the sleeping faces of his two Chinese friends. "They're very dear to you, aren't they? All your friends are."

"Yes."

"Don't feel guilty about not thinking of me. You've been brought up not to dwell on the past. To always look forward. That's what makes you Beck Granger. You know, we've always stood beside you,

Beck – Mum, Dad, me and many angels. Even when you forget me, I won't forget you. You've never been alone. That's faith."

Beck reached out to touch Dian, but then a sudden sound jerked him awake. He sat bolt upright, shaking. Jian and Ju-Long were both asleep.

He couldn't tell if the noise had been another dream thing or an actual noise in the real world. He propped himself up on one elbow and frowned blearily into the darkness. In the absence of firelight, he couldn't make out a thing. The anti-dragon device hadn't moved – there would have been no mistaking that. There was nothing caught in the net. The waves were further off than they had been – in fact (he checked his watch) it was past midnight, so the tide was almost as far out as it could go. Nothing else seemed to have changed, and even though he strained his ears into the night he couldn't hear anything else.

Beck slowly, almost reluctantly, lay back down and allowed his thoughts to drift back into slumber. He prayed that Dian would come to him again in his sleep, in his dream. But she didn't.

In the morning, in the light of a new day, the three of them stood mutely and looked at their trampled collection of water bottles. During the night, a dragon must have felt like having a drink. It couldn't have been after the bottles – it probably just wanted to lick the stone, like the humans had. But in the process, all of the bottles had been tipped over, and a couple were actually punctured by claws from where the dragon had trampled on them.

A seething Ju-Long silently handed the undamaged bottles around, and they each drank what they could from what was left in them. Then she set them up to refill.

Beck thoughtfully rolled one of the punctured bottles in his hand and gazed into the forest. So, they were on an island with creatures that seemed determined to deprive them of food and water.

"You, mate, are becoming a real pain," he murmured.

CHAPTER 19

Breakfast was equipped with a barb – a long, pointed spine, which could cause a nasty injury. It came swimming lazily along the rocky gully of the inlet where Beck had caught last night's dinner, and he knew with one glance that it could kill him if he wasn't careful.

"Whoah," he murmured to himself.

Survivors shouldn't take unnecessary risks – but at the same time, they shouldn't pass opportunities up. He could have waited for something less dangerous. On the other hand, he was hungry.

It was a ray. It had a flat, diamond shaped body about half a metre across, and it moved through the water by gently flapping its two pointed wings. Its eye sockets were a pair of bumps on its top and they reminded Beck of twin gun turrets, panning slowly from side to side.

The barb trailed behind it and it was the ray's main defence. If a predator came too close, it could whip the barb up and stab its attacker, delivering a shot of venom into the bargain. The naturalist Steve Irwin, some years ago, had been killed by a creature like this, Beck remembered. He had swum up behind it and the ray had probably mistaken him for a predator, so it had flipped its sting up and speared him right in the chest.

But Beck's spear was longer than the barb.

So, if I attack from the front, and get it right first time, I should be fine…

He paused, shifted his feet on the rocks to get the right balance, poised – and dived.

Once again, he was blind, guiding himself by sense of direction and gravity. Like the last time, he drove the spear ahead of him with all the weight of his body. He felt the shudder in his arms and shoulders as it grounded against something solid. Had he pinned the ray down? He couldn't see anything and he was aware that somewhere out in that rush of bubbles and blinding salt water, there was a poisonous spine whipping around.

But when he lifted the spear up, he could feel there was something on the end of it, and it wasn't moving. He kicked up to the surface, holding the spear at arm's length, and shook the water from his eyes. And there it was – the ray, draped over the triple prongs, not moving. Its wings and barb hung limply.

"Nice!" he said happily, to no one in particular. "Breakfast is served!"

He headed back to the beach, letting the sun dry him off naturally, with the ray still skewered on the end of the spear.

"Jian?" he asked, looking about when he got there. The other boy was conspicuously not there. Ju-Long had just finished gathering wood for a new fire. There was no sign of dragons.

"I helped him up to the signal point," she said. "He said he is happy to take the watch permanently. He said it is about all he feels able to do, and he does want to be helpful so much."

She noticed him start to frown.

"*And* I left him with a club, in case of dragons, and I set the plastic net up across the narrow part of the point."

"Good job." It sounded like Jian would be safe on his own, but still Beck frowned.

"What is it?"

Beck sighed and decided to share what was on his mind.

"Jian was so full of life when we first met him. Enthusiastic about everything. Now..."

"Think of everything he has been through," Ju-Long said reasonably. "Losing the boat, and then because of his hand it means he cannot be as helpful as he would like."

"Exactly! And I know he didn't sleep well – with all the pain and fretting – and that won't help his state of mind. Basically, I think we should make sure at least one of us is with him, as much as we can, just so he doesn't start to mull over things too much. When you're tired, thirsty or injured, plus feeling guilty, it can be a dangerous cocktail. We need to keep him upbeat."

"I understand. I guess none of us slept well," she admitted. "Dragons on the mind."

"Hm. Yeah." He decided not to let on that he had had a conversation with his dead sister. He took a much-needed drink from one of the refilled water bottles, and held up the food offering.

"We can start by cooking this up there. He's got the fire steel anyway..."

He paused, cocked his head. Had he heard someone shout? A male voice... And there was only one other male on the island.

"Look!" Ju-Long exclaimed. At the same moment, Beck distinctly heard the voice again. It was Jian – but not shouting in alarm. He was shouting to catch attention.

Ju-Long scrambled to her feet. "Come on! Quick!"

From the other side of the island, a column of thick black smoke was rising up above the trees.

CHAPTER 20

The boat was about a kilometre away. It was what Uncle Al would have called a gin palace – three or four decks, sleek and streamlined, white and glittery. The regular throb of its diesel engines came drifting across the water as it cruised slowly by, pitching gently through the waves, probably doing just a fraction of the speed it could make if they let the engines rip.

The signal fire was in full flow, black smoke belching up from the pile of burning flip-flops.

Jian was slumped against a rock, still shouting, in a voice growing hoarser and weaker. He was clutching his injured wrist to his chest and his face was pale. Beck immediately diagnosed what had happened – he somehow managed to light the fire even with his injured hand and he was in agony now.

Jian stopped shouting when he saw Beck and Ju-Long burst from the undergrowth, and just gave a tired nod towards the boat. Ju-Long ran to the very edge of the point and began to jump, waving her arms and shouting in a mixture of Chinese and English.

"Hello! Help! Over here!"

Beck took a moment to check Jian was okay. The older boy's face was sweaty and sheet white, but he reacted to the question on Beck's own face before Beck could say anything.

"I will be all right. Help Ju-Long."

Ju-Long was doing fine, Beck thought. Instead, he ran to the tripod. The fire on the platform was starting to slump down. He found a stick to poke the burning brands back into shape, and to shift the black, molten masses that were the flip-flops back onto the flames. The stink of burning foam was revolting but the black smoke was everything he had hoped for.

Then he hurried back to the undergrowth, and pulled a couple of branches that were thick with leaves off a nearby bush. He dragged them both to the end of the point and tossed one to Ju-Long.

"Here." He heaved his own branch above his head and waved it from side to side.

"*Come on!*" he shouted, with all the force his lungs and throat could manage. "*Over here! Come on!*"

Surely, with the smoke, and the shouting, and the branches – surely they would get the boat's attention now?

Ju-Long redoubled her efforts. Even Jian came to stand alongside them, still half bent over and holding his arm, adding what voice he could to their efforts.

But the boat continued past the island without changing course. Beck could see no one on deck. *Probably all enjoying a lie-in in their air conditioned cabins,* he thought bitterly. He could see even more of the boat's stern now – it was definitely drawing away from them.

He gave the signal fire a final poke, which sent up a last burst of smoke. The embers continued to smoulder but there was no more of the thick black stuff that he had been counting on to attract attention.

He let his branch drop.

Ju-Long had shouted herself hoarse. Her voice died away but she kept waving, until even she had to let it go.

"They didn't see us," she said bitterly.

Beck shot a final look at the boat as it disappeared into the haze. *Maybe they did see us,* he thought. *Maybe they sent off a radio message to the coastguard and they'll be here in a helicopter any time soon...*

But he had to admit he couldn't make himself believe it. The boat hadn't even wiggled a little – they hadn't even wanted to come in closer to have a look at the three people on shore. *They just hadn't been looking.*

Or maybe the people on the boat had seen them, but they thought that letting off black smoke and waving branches at passing vessels was something the locals on these islands did for fun.

There was no point in obsessing about it. What was done, was done.

"Okay," he said heavily. "We'll rebuild the fire and we'll give it another go with the next boat. At least we know boats do come by. Sorry we don't have any more flip-flops, but we'll use extra foliage or some of the packing foam for smoke and that should be almost the same. And meanwhile, I got us some breakfast. You two wait here – I'll go and get it and we can eat it together. Right?"

They looked at him sullenly, but first Jian, then Ju-Long nodded and agreed.

"Right."

"And if you two put a little extra fire in place, we can cook the ray I caught. See you in a few minutes."

Beck hurried back into the undergrowth.

Despite his best intentions, even he couldn't quite put the frustration of the boat out of his mind. No doubt it had a decent radar and radio, so it relied on electronics to pick up any signs of distress, rather than keeping a proper lookout with actual human eyeballs. Which was not something a proper professional sailor would do, but that was how it went –

He stopped, and stared into the distance, not seeing anything except the image in his mind, clear as day.

"Radar!" he exclaimed out loud. "*Duh!* Beck Granger is an idiot!"

Okay, so now he had something else to do. And he would do it, once they had eaten the ray.

Except that when he got back to the beach, the ray had gone. He had left it, well and truly dead, on the platform. There was no way it had come back to life and flapped its way back to the sea. And the really telling piece of forensic evidence was the severed barb, still lying there on the platform. The dragons weren't stupid. They had bitten off the bit they couldn't eat, before stealing the rest.

At least it proved the anti-dragon device and the net had been a sensible idea. The dragons could have got up onto the platform last night, if they had wanted to. In fact, they were big enough to do pretty well what they liked.

He stared into the jungle, looking for the culprit. No reptilian eyes looked back at him.

"Yeah, well, you're not going to win every time," he called with a defiance he didn't feel, "because..." He had to wrack his brains to think of a reason. "There's plenty more food on this island and ultimately we're smarter than you."

He would go fishing again, and then he would put his other bright idea into action. They would get off this island. Beck promised himself this. They were fighters and they would win and survive, despite the setbacks.

But first, he had to catch breakfast. Again. The tide would be too far out by now to use the inlet, but he already knew where he would go this time.

CHAPTER 21

He had spotted the pool the day before, and he had thought of fishing there for breakfast the first time round. But the tide had been so far in that the waves were breaking over the edge, and there would have been a real danger of being bashed against the rocks.

Now the tide was heading out again and the pool stood on its own, with water that was still and clear. He stood on the edge and let his eyes run over the bumps and crevices of the rocky bottom. Clusters of weed clung to the edges, sheltering small colonies of barnacles, mussels and limpets. All of them edible, he thought with satisfaction. But then his eyes settled on the prize. In the very middle of the pool was a large boulder, sitting all on its own, almost like it had been put there as an ornament by an island designer. It was curved so there was shelter beneath it for various forms of sea life. If there was anything more substantial than mussels in the pool, that was there they would be.

He wouldn't know without getting up close and peering through the water. And he had just the thing with him.

"*So - what are you going to do with that?*" Jian had asked, as he and Ju-Long watched Beck cut one of the damaged bottles in half the previous evening.

"*This,*" Beck had said, "*is my Cunning Seeing Device...*"

He had cut a patch off the sheet of transparent plastic that lay in the pile of gathered flotsam, and put the cut-off upper half of the bottle on top of it. Then he had gathered the sides of the loose plastic up around it, tying a loop of net rope around the bottle's neck to hold it all in place.

He was holding it now, together with the sling he had cut for himself out of the plastic netting when he swam out to *Dolphin*, to carry whatever he caught. He slid himself gently into the pool, and lightly kicked himself over to the middle of the water with the Cunning Seeing Device in one hand. He hovered over the central boulder and put the flat end of the Device into the water so that he could peer through the open top of the bottle. He was rewarded with a view of the bottom of the pool, as clear as day. It was the next best thing to having a mask or goggles.

And there they were, nestled under the curve of the boulder. The prize for this pool – clumps of rough-edged grey-brown wedges. Oysters, two or three metres down.

The same laws of physics that applied in diving down to *Dolphin* still applied here: the deeper he went, the more the air in his lungs would be squished and so the less his body would have to take its oxygen from. So, once again he breathed in and out, slowly, deeply, purging the carbon dioxide out of his system. When he felt ready, he left the Cunning Seeing Device floating on the surface and poised himself above the oyster rock. Then he bent double in the water, driving his head and shoulders down and flipping his legs up into the air. With a powerful sweep of his arms he pulled himself down, sliding vertically through the water, navigating by feel and instinct.

His hands brushed against the top of the rock and he felt his way down to where he had seen the oysters. He held onto the rock so that the buoyancy of his air-filled lungs didn't float him back to the surface.

He could feel the oysters, their shells clumped together in tight-packed colonies. The ones to go for were the outliers – the ones in smaller groups, or even sitting on their own. Oyster shells could be razor sharp and they could anchor themselves very firmly to rocks. The bigger the cluster, the greater the chances of slicing his fingers to bits as he tried to pry them loose.

He had to hold each one and rock it back and forth, twisting and turning to break the bond. He could feel them reluctantly peeling off the rock. Each one went into the sling until it was full, and then he kicked his way up to the surface through a cloud of bubbles. He tipped the oysters out onto the rocks, looking around carefully for any marauding dragons that might want a free meal of shellfish, then swam back to the middle of the pool for a second round.

It took two more goes to get a pile that he thought was large enough for breakfast. He was feeling really tired from the exertion, so he decided to call it a day. But he gave the bottom of the pool a last scan with the Cunning Seeing Device.

"Oh, yes!" he breathed.

A lobster the size of his forearm was picking its way across the floor of the pool. A spiny lobster, not the type with claws, which would have made him think twice about having a go. Its segmented body was the colour of burnt orange and it seemed to dance almost daintily across the rocky floor on its eight spindly legs, feeling its way with two massive antennae.

Beck summoned up all the strength he could muster. He left the oysters on the side of the pool and went through his breathing exercises one more time, tracking the lobster's movement as he did it. Then he dived. He pulled himself down to the pool's bottom, swooped the lobster up in his hands, holding onto the back of lobster's shell by its head, and headed back to the surface, all in one movement. He broke the surface with a triumphant *whoop!*

The dangerous part was the tail, which flapped vigorously, but holding it behind the head, Beck was safe. He gave it a whack with a small rock and the lobster stopped moving.

He took the prize up to the signal point personally, to make sure no dragons could get at it. And while Ju-Long and Jian cooked the oysters and lobster on a fire, he got on with his bright idea.

CHAPTER 22

The tide was a little higher this time, when Beck swam back out to *Dolphin*. That just made Beck's job easier. He wasn't diving down this time – he was closer to his target.

He still had to shin a couple of metres up the mast to the crosstrees, sticking out horizontally on either side. Attached to one arm of the crosstrees was *Dolphin*'s radar reflector.

It was made of three metal squares, all intersecting and at right angles to each other, so that it would have fit inside a cube the size of a basketball. And it was dead easy to operate – you didn't have to do anything. The flat metal surfaces, all facing different directions at different angles, gave any radar signals something good and firm to bounce back off.

If they had had this with them on the signal point, maybe that cruiser would have noticed them after all. Even if they didn't keep a human lookout, someone might have noticed the unusually bright signal bouncing back at them.

It took a minute to unscrew the reflector from the shackle that fastened it to the yacht, and then reattach it to a rope that was tied at the other end to the floating life buoy. It would be bad news to drop it now and watch it sink to join the rest of *Dolphin*. He started the swim back to the island, kicking his way with the life buoy looped under his arms and the reflector in both hands.

But the other topic of thought as he kicked his way back to the island was those wretched dragons. He wasn't an expert on reptile thought patterns, but so far they hadn't shown much fear of the three humans, and they seemed to be getting used to thinking of the humans as a handy food source. That was bad. If they had the same outlook as many animals then their sense of expectation could change to a feeling of entitlement. Like those seagulls infesting British coastal towns, which have come to expect that humans would feed them and can turn aggressive if they don't.

The basic anti-dragon device wouldn't be enough if they got more insistent, and they didn't want to have to live on the platform permanently. There might be enough net to surround an area of the beach – but he wanted to use the net for other things. No, the friends would have to think about building some kind of stockade – a permanent fence that the dragons couldn't get through. It would have to be really sturdy – even if it was moderately strong, the dragons would be heavy enough to get through it if they threw their weight against it.

Problem was, Beck didn't know exactly what the dragons *could* do. They could probably swim, so if they built the stockade around the camp, they would have to include all directions, even the sea. Alternatively, they could shift their camp to an easily defended bit of land, like the signal point, which could only be approached from one direction. But then – well, even if they blocked off the land approach, could the dragons climb the point's sheer sides? Beck wouldn't be surprised – they seemed hardcore enough. Everything you expected, they did something different.

Back on the island, he hurried up to the signal point. A breakfast of oysters and cooked lobster was calling his name.

"Woah!"

He emerged from the undergrowth and found himself staring at two very hostile-looking friends – heavy sticks in their hands, poised and ready to attack, waiting the other side of the plastic net that Ju-Long had set up as a barrier across the neck of land joining point and island.

"Only me?" he added with a hopeful smile. Between them they managed to crack a smile in return, and relax.

"We thought you were a dragon," Jian admitted.

"Well, I am as hungry as a dragon – that's for sure."

As Ju-Long set about cooking the lobster over the fire, Beck showed them the radar reflector and described his ideas about building a decent dragon defence.

"A stockade?" Jian asked.

"Or something like it. Something stronger than this."

Beck paced by the net. It was bright orange, and tough, so it might deter dragons if they weren't too determined. Problem was, it wouldn't stop them if they worked out that hey, it was only plastic.

The radar reflector now hung from a tree, the rebuilt signal fire was ready to go, the lobster was cooking nicely in its shell – all was well. For the moment. It was never too late to adapt your plans. And frankly, moving camp up here might be the best course.

Beck looked thoughtfully at the ground beneath his feet. It was the narrowest part of the signal point, only a couple of metres across, but building a fence that was long enough to cover that distance, and high and strong enough to deter dragons, would still take a lot of wood.

Of course, they had quite a bit of wood down on the beach, in the form of the platform. Which meant that the platform would have to be dismantled. And the water bank was down there ...

"Too many options, and I'm hungry," he muttered. He went to join them and sit by the fire. "Thing is," he said as he sat down, "we don't know how long we're going to be here, and they're losing their fear of us, if they ever had any. We don't even know how many there are, but ..."

"At least four," Ju-Long said slowly, looking past them.

Beck looked round.

Four dragons had emerged from the bushes and they stood where he had just been, at the neck of the signal point. The smell of cooking lobster must have lured them out.

Each one was the length of an adult human and about the same weight, with teeth and claws and jaws that could inflict serious damage. Chew through flesh, quite probably crunch a bone.

Two of them hissed at the humans and then, with the friends' escape route blocked, the four of them started to walk forwards. They trampled the plastic net without even noticing it, and kept coming.

CHAPTER 23

"**N**o!" Beck shouted. "Back away!"

The way their bodies hung from their leg sockets gave the dragons a swagger, like gunslingers strolling down the street, knowing that they were boss and no one could do anything about it.

He had stood up to wild animals in the past. Often the trick was to make yourself look and sound big and scary, and then hope they decide it's not worth the trouble and go away.

So he raised his arms and lunged at them, yelling, "Aarrgh!"

Reptile brains don't work the same way as mammalian ones. They weren't scared. The nearest dragon stopped and looked at him. It gave another hiss, and a snap of its jaws. Beck quickly jumped back out of range.

Ju-Long had picked up the piece of wood that Jian had chosen for defence while he stood watch. She banged it hard against the ground in front of one of the dragons and shouted at it. This one also stopped to think about what to do, while the others kept moving.

She lifted it up, and its head flashed forward. Its jaws seized on the wood, and held it firm. She tugged on it with both hands but, try as she might, she couldn't pull it free.

Endangered species or not, enough was enough. With another shout, Beck loosed a kick at the nearest dragon to him. His foot thudded into its muscular side. It merely turned its head and looked at him. Beck tried again, and then a third time. The dragon snapped at his foot – a reminder that said, *look, I've got a bite that could kill you and you haven't.*

It was the slowest fight Beck had ever been in. The dragons didn't pounce and jump like a predatory mammal would have. If the friends had somewhere to run to, the dragons could have run after them. But, cornered like this, the dragons seemed to think they had all the time in the world. They were fast when they lunged and snapped, but otherwise they never broke out of a slow stroll. And they just kept coming.

Jian pulled a piece of wood that burned at one end from the fire – about the one thing he could do single handed – and waved it in the face of the dragon nearest to him. For the first time, one of the dragons looked thoughtful. It had probably never seen fire before, but it must have sensed the heat of the flame and realised it could be hurt. It stopped, and it didn't bite at the wood. A couple of times it made an effort to nip the waving brand, but every time it sensed the fire and stopped. Boy and dragon were at an impasse.

"Okay! Fire!" Beck shouted. He pulled a piece of his own from the pile. It seemed weird to be fighting dragons with fire, but hey, if that was what it took...

But there were only three of them, and four dragons. Even if they each stopped one of the creatures, there was always one more to press forward. Ju-Long had a burning brand of her own, and she thrust it in the face of the fourth dragon that was trying to bypass her. But immediately the third dragon took a couple of steps forward.

Slowly, but surely, the four dragons were advancing down the point, pressing the four friends backwards. They were almost level with the fire and the thing they were after – the cooking lobster. Beck almost snatched it away from the fire, but then realised that would only lure them further. As long as it was cooking over the flames, it was safe – the dragons wouldn't make a grab for it.

The dragons seemed to have realised it too. They gathered by the fire and looked at it longingly. Their tongues flickered in and out, almost too fast for the eye to see, as they sampled the smell of cooking shellfish in the air and felt the heat of the flames on their faces. The two lines, humans and dragons, seemed to have come to a halt.

"Keep watching," Beck said. "Don't move back. If they can't get the lobster ..."

"They might decide to try one of us," Ju-Long agreed.

None of them put their bits of wood down or took their eyes off the lizards.

And there things might have stayed, until perhaps the fire burnt out and the way was clear for one of the dragons to grab the lobster. But the dragon at the end of the line grew impatient, and lashed its tail. The tip caught one of the legs of the signal tripod and the whole structure spun around. It wobbled, tilting on just two legs, as if it couldn't decide to go with gravity or not.

After half a second that felt like a year, it slowly topped back onto its third leg. Beck almost breathed a sigh of relief. But the tripod's momentum made it tilt over onto another pair of legs. The dragon that had lashed its tail, maybe surprised itself, snapped at him and thumped at it with its tail again, just as it was its most precarious on two legs only. Unbalanced, the whole structure toppled over the edge of the point.

"*No!*" Beck bellowed. He heard the sound of wood falling against the rocks below. "You stupid ..."

Then Ju-Long cried out in alarm, "Jian!"

But it was too late. Jian, distracted by the collapse of the tripod, had let the end of his burning branch drop. The dragon that he had been holding at bay lunged, not at the hand holding the wood but at his other one, the injured one in the sling. He screamed as its jaws closed over his wrist and dragged him down to the ground.

Crunch.

CHAPTER 24

"**G**et off him!"
Beck clubbed his stick as hard as he could against the dragon's side and Ju-Long launched a furious kick at its head. But the dragon had already let go of Jian's wrist and backed off.

Now none of the humans were distracting the other dragons, and the other three all pressed forward. One of them swung around, maybe looking for the food it could still smell, and its tail knocked against the base of the fire. It quickly flicked the tail away again when it sensed the heat, but the pieces of wood scattered and the skewer that held the lobster over the flames toppled to the ground. A dragon swiftly swooped and grabbed it in its jaws, pulling it away from the heat. Another dragon pounced and grabbed the lobster's head. The shell split in two, leaving each of them with half a lobster. The other two dragons immediately started to grapple with their friends, with hisses and strange croaks of frustration. For the time being, they had forgotten the humans and Beck could give all his attention to Jian.

The older boy lay on the ground, eyes closed, shuddering, with a strange, choking sound coming from his mouth – the sound of someone in so much pain that it couldn't come out all at once. Dreading what he was going to see, Beck gently took his wrist and studied it – and blinked when he found hardly any damage at all.

The splint on Jian's arm bore the clear imprint of a powerful pair of jaws, but it had also taken all the impact. No wonder the dragon had dropped him so quickly – it had expected a tasty morsel and just got wood and polystyrene. The pressure would have squeezed the ends of Jian's broken bone together, and Beck could well imagine the pain that must have caused. But that was all.

But just as he was feeling a gush of relief, and opening his mouth to tell Jian that he would be okay, a flash of red appeared. And grew. Blood was pooling along the edge of the splint.

Beck gently turned Jian's wrist over, and cursed under his breath as he took the whole picture in. The splint had protected the top and bottom of Jian's wrist – but, on the side, just below the wrist joint, the dragon's teeth had torn through the skin. Blood welled up out of the puncture wounds, each about a centimetre wide. There was no way of telling how deep they went. And they would need attention. If they were back in civilisation, any kind of animal bite would mean heading straight off to the nearest hospital.

No hospitals here, though.

"Come on. Let's go," he said quietly, shooting a final look at the squabbling dragons. They were aggravated – they might easily just turn on the humans. He quickly picked up the sling full of oysters. Beck wasn't going to let them go to waste. "Jian, can you stand? Ju-Long, help me..."

It wasn't easy because Jian was taller than both of them, and he was still faint with pain. His mind was jumbled, and every conscious and unconscious thought was about doing absolutely nothing that might jar his body with the tiniest movement. But they helped him to his feet and supported him with arms around his waist. They staggered past the dragons, which were still fighting even though the lobster had completely gone.

"I feel sick," Jian mumbled. His face was whiter than Beck had ever seen.

"We need to treat those bites," he said. "Any kind of animal bite can be infectious and goodness knows what's in those things' saliva. We don't know what they've been eating."

They had already set up a fire back at the beach camp, ready to be lit when they returned that evening. Jian was ready to slump down on the sand, but Beck shook his head. They helped him over to the platform so that he could prop himself up there, with his arm resting on the wood. It wasn't exactly sterile hospital conditions but it was cleaner than the sand.

"Brace yourself. I'm going to take the splint off..."

As gently as he could, Beck undid the ropes that held Jian's splint in place. The two halves came away cleanly and he could study the rest of Jian's arm. He breathed a sigh of relief when he saw there were no more bites – just the two he already knew about. They were circular puncture wounds, so if they didn't go bad, they had the best chance of healing nicely.

"Okay." Beck handed Ju-Long the metal saucepan and a bottle. "Fill these up with sea water, please."

Ju-Long nodded and hurried off, as Beck bent down to light the fire. For once, being stranded on an island was in their favour. They were close to sea, and salt water was naturally antiseptic.

Ju-Long was back. She hastened over to Jian and began to dribble salt water from the bottle slowly over the bite marks, rinsing anything larger than a bacterium out of the wounds. The water mingled with the blood that was already clotting and ran to the ground in red streams.

Beck balanced the full saucepan over the fire and willed the flames to take hold so that the water could start to boil. Which of course, he thought, a watched pot never does. A wood fire was great for roasting food but it wasn't as hot, or as quick, as a gas fire back home.

"Is there anything in the bite marks?" he asked. "Any black specks? Bits of dragon food or anything else?"

"No," Ju-Long reported after a moment. "They seem clean. I will keep washing them."

"Yes, keep going, thanks."

While he was waiting for the water to boil, he took the knife and cut a strip off Jian's trouser leg, from ankle up to the knee. He dunked the material in the slowly warming water. The wounds would need bandaging, and the bandage would need disinfecting if it wasn't just going to add to the problem.

Tendrils of steam were curling up from the water, and small bubbles were appearing, clinging to the sides of the saucepan. He gave the bandage a prod with the knife blade to push it all under water.

Finally, the water in the pan was heaving and bubbling. He gave it a minute, then carried the knife and pan over to Jian.

He lifted the bandage out of the boiling water with a stick and held it so that the air would cool it down. When he thought enough time has passed, he lowered the bandage onto Jian's wrist and wrapped it around the bite marks. Jian grunted, a sound of a much deeper pain pushing its way out. His arm was still unsplinted; the ends of the broken bones were rubbing together.

CHAPTER 25

Ju-Long quickly wrapped the bandage around Jian's wrist, tying the ends together in a reef knot. Only then did Jian let himself make a sound.

"*Ah-h-h-h...*"

It came out like a release of steam under colossal pressure.

Beck quickly tied the splint back onto Jian's arm. Jian cradled it tenderly.

"You've done what you can. Thank you."

"But, what next?" Ju-Long said in frustration. "The dragons take another meal! We need to guard against them properly –"

"I don't think we can," Beck said quietly. He shoved his hands into his pockets and went to stand looking out to sea – and at the next island, a kilometre away. "We talked about a stockade, we talked about using the net – but face it, they're strong enough to push through any kind of defences that we build. We could – *could* – try to kill them. Yeah, I know," he added in response to Ju-Long's surprised look. "Endangered and all that, and this is me speaking, but there's still more of them in this world than there are of us. But we don't know if there are only the four we saw, and we don't know how fast they could move if they really felt threatened. Jian was lucky to be bitten where he was. A bite like that on one of our arms or legs and we'd be out of the game for good."

"So what do you suggest?" Ju-Long asked.

Jian had already seen where Beck was looking.

"You think we are on the wrong island," he said.

"Yeah, I do."

Ju-Long followed Beck's gaze.

"There may be dragons there too," she pointed out. "Perhaps ours swam over from there?"

It had already crossed Beck's mind.

"Best case scenario – there's no dragons. Worst case – there's dragons, but the island's much bigger and we'll have more space and more resources to defend against them. Which we don't have here." He shot a final look across the water. "Either way, we need to evacuate."

CHAPTER 26

"So," Jian said, "we get to make a raft after all. Tiangong-4."

It was good to see Jian willing to make a joke, even if it was a little close to the bone. Beck managed a small smile.

He and Beck stood and surveyed the results of several hours' effort. The raft sat on the sand at the edge of the water, loaded up with a pile of their few possessions, waiting for them.

It had been a cooperative effort for all three of them – Beck and Ju-Long doing most of the work but always with Jian being as useful as he could be. He could hold ropes steady while someone else tied them, and he could gather things together with one hand, ready to come with them on the journey.

They had worked without a break for the rest of the morning, with only a slight pause for a lunch of raw oysters – not great, but quicker than catching and cooking another fish. They had to get everything ready so that they could make the magic target of 1pm, when the tide would be fully out. Jian calculated the incoming tide would help them on their way. Going against the tide would just be a waste of effort – no matter how strongly they pushed forward, the weight of an entire ocean would be pushing them back, and that would only have one result, sweeping them out into the South China Sea.

The raft was built of three layers: a basic framework of driftwood, followed by the lifebuoys and all the polystyrene packaging they could find, followed by another layer of wood for Jian to sit on. Most of the wood had come from dismantling the platform and the rest came from plundering the reserves of flotsam washed up on the shoreline.

The raft was small, so the plan was for Jian to sit on it with their things, and he and Ju-Long would swim behind it and push.

The raft did have a mast, of sorts – a single upright piece of wood that would be higher than Jian when he was sitting down. Beck had tied the radar reflector to the top of this, to make them more visible – not just to ships far off, but to any that might come sailing through the channel between islands – and then draped a couple of layers of what was left of the rope fishing net over it, so that it covered the raft like a very holey tent.

"That will not keep the rain off," Jian had commented wryly.

"It's not meant to." Beck lifted a corner of the net up to show him. The deck of the raft was dappled with points of light. "It'll be like sitting under a tree – it cuts out about fifty percent of the sun." He looked out over the blue, sparkling waves. "And you'll need it. It'll be blistering out there."

Ju-Long came down the beach towards them.

"All done," she said.

Back where the camp had been, at the top of the beach and above the high-water mark, she had done the last thing they would do on this island – use stones to mark out a large arrow, pointing out to sea and over at their destination. She had also written their names in the sand:

LI JU-LONG
ZHOU JIAN
BECK GRANGER

Anyone who came looking for them should certainly work out where they had been and where they had gone.

"Everyone have a drink." Beck passed the bottles around. "Might as well carry it inside us." They each drained one bottle – the rest were all stored on top of the raft.

He gave a last look at the camp, and forced a laugh.

"Aw, that's sweet. They've come to say goodbye."

A couple of dragons prowled around where the camp had been.

"Or, they are asking 'where's my fish?'" Ju-Long said.

Beck shrugged. "Whichever. Come on, let's go."

He and Ju-Long dragged the raft out into the sea. Jian waded out and clambered awkwardly onto it, making himself as comfortable as he could in the middle. Ju-Long and Beck began to push.

The first wave came at them before the water was up to their chests. The raft rose up, with Jian clinging on, and the water broke around them. The raft splashed down into the trough of water behind the wave and bubbles foamed up through the cracks. But the life buoys and foam in the second layer were extremely buoyant, and even though Jian got soaked the raft rose up out of the water again with ease.

Beck felt his body getting lighter and lighter on his feet, and the next wave lifted him off the sea floor altogether. They were further out, so the wave wasn't as high, and the raft rose up and down without difficulty. With feet churning behind them, he and Ju-Long propelled the raft away from the island of the dragons.

CHAPTER 27

"Ninety eight," Jian called over the sound of splashing water. "Ninety nine...a hundred!"

Beck and Ju-Long gratefully stopped swimming and clung to the edge of the raft. Against his better judgement, Beck looked back.

The old island was still disappointingly near. Even after only five minutes – and a hundred kicks – Beck's legs felt like lumps of lead dangling from his waist.

With his head at sea level and the raft in the way, he couldn't tell how close the next island looked. If at all. He decided not to bother. They would get there when they got there – if it took a long time then it would be what he expected, and if it was sooner then that would be a nice reward.

Jian passed a couple of water bottles down under the edge of the net that shielded the raft. Beck took his carefully to keep salt splashes out and drank a couple of mouthfuls, making sure that every drop washed around the inside of his mouth before swallowing.

"Okay, let's get going again," he said as he and Ju-Long handed their bottles back up. His legs still felt like dead weight, but maybe there was a little more life in them as he began to kick and the raft carried on in its journey.

"One." Jian began counting again. "Two, three..."

They swam for two more hundred-kick stints without any trouble. Jian navigated from his perch on the raft, since Ju-Long and Beck couldn't see where they were going. "Go left a bit ... that's it ..."

They had their third break and drink of water, and resumed.

As Jian was reaching a hundred for the fourth time, Beck felt the raft jump suddenly. Instead of forwards it went up, then backwards, and he had to push it away to stop it hitting him in the face.

"Woah! What?"

"Rough water –" Jian began. The raft reared again, and Beck heard the gasp as Jian fell badly on his side.

"Are you okay?"

"Yes –"

Water broke over them all.

Beck looked to left and right, past the raft. The water that had been rising and falling in large swells had suddenly become choppy and agitated.

"It is the tide," Jian reported. "There must be two currents colliding here. The waves are quite high."

"No kidding," Beck muttered. This was something they couldn't have seen from the island, or even from very far away. Not until they were right on top of it. He kept a hold on the raft. It would be all too easy to become separated and unable to grab it again. They would be carried away by wind and currents.

"Is it going to push us off course?" he asked.

"Maybe not. But ..." Jian clutched at the raft as it dipped again. "It could tip us over if we do not keep moving."

Ju-Long and Beck glanced at each other.

"No break this time?" she said.

"I guess not," he said grimly. "Not until we're through it ..."

Spluttering as water broke over their heads, arms now aching just as much as their legs as they grappled with the bucking raft, they continued on their way.

It's only a kilometre, Beck kept telling himself. *It's only a stupid kilometre...*

He could walk a kilometre. He could probably hop a kilometre without taking a break. He could definitely swim one – up and down the school pool ten times, no problem. But this was different. It used so many different muscles – your arm muscles to keep your arms up and push the raft, your neck muscles to hold your head out of the water, your stomach and waist muscles to keep your body straight, and of course your leg muscles to do all the heavy work. Kick, kick, kick... And the water itself didn't help – its up and down motion only increased the distance they had to swim. The waves constantly knocked them one way or another, so they constantly had to adjust their direction, and although the tide carried them mostly in the right way, they kept having to alter course or they would have been swept right past the island altogether...

Beck had known it would be mentally and physically taxing. Anything to do with the sea always was, if you were relying on your own efforts. It had infinite strength and variety to throw at you, and humans only had the strength of their own bodies and the limits of their own minds to respond with.

But... *this* taxing...

Kick, kick, kick...

On their seventh – or was it eighth? – break, suddenly the island was looking much closer. Beck could see it ahead, even from his position with his head at the same level of the sea, behind the raft.

"Okay! One more go and we're there!"

And, soon after they set off for that last final push with legs that felt like they would drop off at any moment, Beck heard the sound of surf. He began to feel the surges in the water, pulling on his body. The raft, and them with it, began to move smoothly and slowly up and down as it encountered the swell that would become waves. The motion become heavier and more urgent.

"Here we go ..." Jian called.

Beck felt the raft moving of its own volition, no longer pushed by him but carried forward by water rushing towards the beach. The surf sounds grew louder and he felt the vibration carried through the water.

And suddenly they were on the top of a wave. There was no controlling the raft's progress now. White water surged all around them as they rushed towards the new island. Beck braced himself for another rough landing ...

CHAPTER 28

The raft shuddered and shook as it grounded, and white water rushed all around and over them. Beck felt his body scrape against the sand. He propped himself up on his knees, though the new effort made him grunt and groan, as the water streamed away again.

He swept his eyes up and down the beach of their new home. He had already known this island would be larger than the last one. The beach was a sandy stretch – proper sand, not gravel like the last one – that was wrapped around the base of the island like a skirt. There was plenty of sand beyond the high water mark, followed by rising ground covered with shrubs and bushes and trees. Unlike the last island, most of this one would always be above the water even at high tide.

But there would be time for exploring later. Right now, Beck could hear a fresh wave gathering strength behind him.

"C'mon," he grunted, "before the next one..."

He and Ju-Long staggered to their feet and helped Jian clamber out from beneath the net. Together they dragged the raft up the beach. The wave caught them before they were all the way up, but it only surged around their knees and they hung onto the raft easily as it bobbed in the foam. The wave actually made it easier for them, carrying the raft a little bit further up the sand before the water ran out again.

Once the raft was above the high water mark, as though there had been some unseen signal, all three of them sank down onto it with a sigh. They sat side by side and looked across the water, back at the island they had abandoned.

Jian was cradling his injured arm, which he often did, but he looked more drawn than usual.

"Are you all right?" Ju-Long asked.

The older boy nodded wearily.

"I am." He sounded as tired as Beck felt. "But I am not looking forward to having to start all over again."

"Well, it's not completely from scratch," Beck pointed out. He jerked a thumb back at the pile of goods on the raft. "We have all this. And this place is bigger." He stretched his neck to look from left to right behind them. "Doesn't look as rocky so we'll have to fish in a different way." A crab scuttled past his toes – a tiddler, barely the size of his palm. "Okay, the crabs are weedy, but there's bound to be more animal life, probably ones we can eat, and probably more water too."

"As long as the animal life is not more dragons," Ju-Long said grimly.

"Well, if it is, we'll have more to protect ourselves with – *Ow.*"

He slapped at his neck at the sudden feel of something jabbing there, like Jian had decided to stick a pin into him when his head was turned. He inspected his hand. There was nothing there but he already knew what it was.

"And part of the animal life is sandflies," he said with a sigh. There would be no protecting against them. They were only about half a centimetre long, and they moved so fast they were practically invisible, but they packed a punch like several mosquitoes all rolled into one. The bite on his neck would be red and itchy before he knew it, and if they stayed down here on the beach they would soon be covered with scratchy lumps.

"We need to get away from the sand. Let's see what else this place has."

"I will...stay a while. Risk the sandflies. You two go," Jian said. Beck shot him a look. Jian was sitting, slightly bent over, still cradling his wrist. His face was pale and sweaty – and it was sweat that had come up since they arrived, not just splashes of sea water from their journey. Beck wondered if the splinted bones had maybe broken loose, rubbing against each other...

"Is it getting worse? I could resplint it –"

"Perhaps. Perhaps." Jian forced a smile. "But not now. I am just...tired, and exploring the island will be more tiring. Is there anything I could do here on the beach?"

"Well, if you're sure..." Beck looked back at the trees beyond the beach. If the island was uninhabited by humans, there would be no natural paths, no clear areas for one-handed people to walk through without having to pick their way. Jian had a point. "Okay. If you don't mind being bitten, you could spell out 'S.O.S.' in the sand? Using nice, big characters. As big as you can get."

"That, I can do," Jian agreed gratefully. "And with this –" He nodded at his hand. "I think a few bites will make no difference to how I feel."

Considering everything Jian, and especially Jian's hand, had been through, Beck could understand the boy feeling drained. But he would check on the hand later – resplint the wrist, and put a freshly boiled bandage on the dragon bite.

"Come on," he said to Ju-Long. "Let's see what we've got."

CHAPTER 29

"I think he is hurting more than he will admit," Ju-Long said anxiously, once they were out of earshot. She and Beck picked their way through closely packed trees and bushes, following the slope of the ground upwards. Beck wanted to find the island's highest point, like he had on the last one, so he could make a map in his mind of how things lay. After that, he could plan.

This would have been a much better island to be wrecked on, he had already decided glumly. The basic geology had to be the same, but all the rocks here were buried beneath sand and earth. The soil was richer than on the last island, and obviously deeper and better watered, which made it able to support the plant life around them. Which meant there was a good chance of water somewhere – water that pooled instead of just draining away into trickles.

"I'm sure of it," he agreed. "And if I was in his place, I probably wouldn't be admitting it either."

"Boys!" she exclaimed in frustration, and he grinned.

"Yeah, that's part of it. And part of it is not wanting to be a burden, and part of it is knowing there's nothing anyone can do about his hand anyway. Well, apart from cutting it off altogether."

She looked sideways at him.

"Please tell me that was an English joke."

"It was an English joke."

"Thank you. English jokes are not funny." But she still gave Beck a smile.

The ground ahead of them levelled out, and almost immediately dropped down again. Beck stopped and looked from left to right. It looked like this was the island's highest point – in fact, a ridge ran along the entire length of it. The island was shaped like a giant wedge pointing upwards, and everything was either one side or the other of the thin end. He cocked his head and looked along the ridge with interest. An animal trail ran along it.

Ju-Long hadn't noticed, but Beck knew the signs to look for. The way fallen leaves were disturbed, small branches bent, the ground was trodden down, and all in a thin line. That was worth knowing. He was praying it wasn't dragons.

The trees were too close together for him to see far in any direction.

"Wait here a mo," he said. He picked the thickest tree he could see, one that looked like it wouldn't bend under his weight, and quickly shinned up it, holding himself against the trunk with the pressure of his knees, pulling himself up with his hands, moving his knees up, and repeating. In a few moments he was level with the branches. He pulled himself up to stand on the one that looked the sturdiest, holding himself up with a hand on the trunk, and moved the leaves aside to peer through.

In one direction was the dragon island. In the other, Beck could see a couple more islands, and maybe the hint of a third beyond them. None of the islands were as close as the dragon one, so they wouldn't be heading on to them, he thought, unless there was a *really* good reason. And he really hoped there wouldn't be.

He took a couple more moments to make his observations, then started to climb down. One last thing caught his eye. The sea was still blue and sparkling beneath a clear sky, but a dark line to the south east suggested there was a different kind of weather below the horizon. Beck didn't know if it would be coming their way or not. If it was then it would take at least a day to arrive, whatever it was.

He climbed quickly back down to the ground and dusted his hands on his trousers. Ju-Long was waiting with a big smile.

"Do you want to see what I found while you were up there?"

She led him away, but only a few metres, downslope from the ridge. His eyes lit up when he saw what she was talking about.

"Oh, yes!"

It was a dry furrow in the ground, slightly ragged, like someone had dug it out with a trowel. It was obviously well established, not recently made. The earth was dry and it was full of dead leaves. It seemed to start from nowhere and head off into the trees down the slope.

But there was only one thing that could have made it, and that was running water. The ridge was the island's watershed. Rain ran off it in one direction or another, and this was obviously one of the channels it used, carved out over probably hundreds of years.

"Let's see where it goes ..."

They followed it for five minutes before the ground levelled off. A natural bump in the slope of the ridge created a flat ledge with a dimple in the middle, and in the dimple was a pool.

It wasn't the kind either of them wanted to dive into. It must have been recharged with rainwater during the typhoon, and that had only been a week ago, but it wasn't what you would call fresh. Leaves had blown in and rotted; animals would have peed and pooed in it too. But, it was the nicest sight Beck had seen for a long time.

"Hey, don't worry," Beck said when he saw Ju-Long's look of disappointment. "It might be the only water on the island, but it'll be fine if we filter it and boil it. So, we can set up camp here and have a water bank going, and ... hello ..."

His attention was caught by something on the ground. Marks in the soil. He knelt down to touch them and Ju-Long stepped forward to see what it was. Just then the bushes across from the pool suddenly rustled. They looked up sharply.

The bush rustled again and there was the sound of something large moving away.

"Oh, no," Ju-Long breathed. "Not more dragons!"

CHAPTER 30

The bush rustled again. Beck had the feeling of being watched by careful, suspicious eyes.

"No," he said thoughtfully, "these aren't dragons."

He had known what it was when he saw the soil marks by the edge of the pool, pressed into the soft, damp mud. And the breeze carried a distinctly mammalian, farmyard smell towards him. He couldn't have identified the animal from the smell alone, but the marks were the giveaway. Each one was a pair of indentations, side by side as if he had pressed his first two fingers into the ground, over and over again. He tapped them to show what he meant.

"These are pig footprints. There are wild pigs on this island. They must come here to drink."

And he would bet it was pigs that had created the animal track along the ridge. They must use it as their personal highway along the island – high ground, looking down on both sides, with a good view of any predators. But there couldn't be any predators on this island, because if there were on an island this size, there wouldn't be any pigs at all. Which meant the pigs were the top life form – or had been, until the three of them had arrived.

"As far as I know," Ju-Long said thoughtfully, "pigs are not endangered."

"Not generally." He grinned, and looked at the bushes that hid the pig. They moved again, but only because the pig was sniffing around and moving away.

He ran in his head through what they needed to do, and the time it would take. It was mid-afternoon. Could they squeeze everything into the last four hours of daylight?

Yes, he decided, they could. They *would*.

"We'll bring everything up here for our camp to be near the water." There might be mosquitoes, he thought, but that was inevitable anywhere on the island, and it was better than sand-flies. "Then we'll build another signal fire down on the beach – there's nowhere clear up here we can use for a signal point, so the beach is the next best thing. And then, we can see what we can do to help us survive a little longer!"

* * *

The tree was three metres tall and it stood next to the pig trail. Its trunk was just right and Beck could get both his hands around it. It wasn't so thick that he couldn't pull it down to the ground, and it wasn't so thin that it just snapped if he tried.

And when he did, and let go, it sprang back up into the air to stand upright again.

Perfect.

Catching a pig, even on an island this size, would be a big chal-lenge. He was the only one of the three of them with any hunting experience, and even if the island wasn't exactly *big*, it was big *enough*.

So, the pigs had to be trapped. And thanks to the trail, he knew where a trap could be set.

Ju-Long had cut a length of rope with a slip knot at one end. She fed the other end of the rope back through the knot's loop, and now the rope was a noose. A pig that blundered into it would pull the rope through the knot and make it tighter.

But there was always the chance it could just pull itself free again. To make extra sure it stayed caught, it had to be lifted off the ground – and that was where the tree came in.

Beck cut a notch in the stem of a sapling that grew next to the trail. He tied a loop in one end of a piece of rope, and tied the other end of the rope around the tree. Then he heaved the tree down with both hands, straining as he fought the tree's desire to return upright, and hooked the loop into the notch. The rope stretched taut, but it held and the tree stayed bent over.

It needed to be tested. He stood back a safe distance and gave the rope an experimental prod with a length of wood. It slid out of the notch and the tree whipped itself smartly upright, yanking the wood out of his hand.

Okay, he decided, that would do.

He pulled the tree back down again and fastened it again with the rope back in the notch. Then he tied the free end of the snare to the tree a little higher up, laid the loop gently down on the ground, and covered it up with a scattering of leaves. The pig would come blundering through and knock the tree free without realising it was standing in the snare. The tree would whip itself upright. The snare would close around the pig, or at least one of its legs, and lift it up.

That was the theory.

He had to be absolutely sure, of course, that the pig would stand in that precise spot. That was what Ju-Long was doing now. He went to help her.

For a distance of ten metres on either side of the snare, and up to a height of about one metre, Ju-Long was lashing the branches of the undergrowth together. Some she tied with net rope, some she just twined together. From a distance it looked untouched, but any animal that tried to run through it, expecting to push the branches apart, wouldn't be able to. Animals took the path of least resistance unless they had a good reason not to. Ju-Long and Beck would build a barrier like this on either side of the trail, angled towards the snare, and the pig would find itself funnelled towards the trap. The killing zone.

The barriers were in place; the trap was set. Beck checked his watch. They had about an hour of daylight left. Getting across from the last island, then exploring this one, and then setting the trap, had taken up a good chunk of day. If they were going to do this today, they needed to act now. Not that it would be the end of the world if they waited until tomorrow, but roast pork tonight would be good.

"Ready?" he asked. Ju-Long nodded. He checked his watch. "Be in position in five minutes, then go for it."

"Five minutes." Ju-Long set the alarm on her own watch. "Understood." She turned to go.

"Wait, hang on a moment!" Beck called. She looked back, and he handed her a thick, sturdy stick. She flashed him a smile of understanding and took it, then carried on her way. The whole point of what they were about to do was to spook a pig to run into the trap – but spooked animals can turn nasty on whoever is spooking them. Even domesticated farm pigs could get aggressive if they were angry, and this would be a wild animal, not domesticated at all. It would have teeth and, if it was a male, it would have tusks – sharp ones, too, every bit as dangerous as a dragon's bite.

She would need protection.

Beck didn't have a stick – he had a spear. They had brought the triple-pointed spear with them from the old island, but this island wasn't suitable for diving in rock pools, so he had modified it. First he had cut a slot in one end and wrapped rope tight around it to stop the slot from splitting the shaft further down. Then he had opened his knife's sharp cutting blade up and wedged the handle into the slot, tying more rope to hold it firmly in place. The blade pointed outwards, and with the point on the end, it would be a lethal weapon.

He picked the spear up and turned to head in the other direction, picking his way through the undergrowth down his side of the ridge. By the time he and Ju-Long reached the beach they would be on opposite sides of the island.

Beck emerged onto the sand and quickly turned right, hurrying along until he estimated he was about half way to the island's end. Ju-Long should be in a similar position on her side. He checked his watch again. There was a minute to go.

He turned to face the jungle and drew in some slow breaths. In many places around the world, indigenous people would ask permission or blessing of the spirits for a hunt. And so he sent out a prayer to the forest of the island.

Lord, thank you for providing us with this food. Help us to make a clean kill. Beck paused. "Amen!"

And the silence gave the trees time to settle down and for quiet to return.

Thirty seconds. He took a grip on the spear. Twenty seconds. Ten ... Time. The hunt was on.

CHAPTER 31

"Okay!" Beck said, but not loudly. "Any pigs on this island better get out of our way because I'm coming through!"

He began to walk forward, pushing back into the undergrowth, bumping the ground and trees with the shaft of the spear as he went.

They didn't want to set up a mighty racket that would spook every creature on the island. You never knew what you would get running into the trap then. But they made enough noise to make it clear that two largish mammals were coming through. Other animals would deal with it in different ways.

Birds would fly off, circle round, and land back in their trees. Small animals would cower deeper in their hiding places and wait for the noise to go away. And big animals would move away from it.

By approaching from different directions at the end of the island, Ju-Long and Beck were sealing that end of the island off as a possible refuge. The pigs would head inland, which meant uphill, which meant going along their track towards the barriers...

That was, assuming they didn't get so annoyed that they decided to attack the source of the noise instead. The thought of a pair of razor-sharp tusks was still foremost in Beck's mind, and while he banged the spear and used it to make noise, he also kept both hands on it and ran his eyes ceaselessly over the undergrowth around him, always on the lookout for a hundred kilos of angry sausage meat charging at him.

And then a new noise came screeching through the trees – a high pitched squealing. It was definitely not from a human throat, and there was only one reason a pig would be making it. The trap had been sprung.

Beck hurried forwards, pushing his way through clumps of bushes, guided by the sounds. There were two reasons to hurry. Just in case the noose was loose in any way, he didn't want the pig to get away – and assuming it had worked exactly as he intended, he didn't want the pig to suffer either.

He made the top of the ridge and hurried along the trail towards the sound. Ju-Long emerged from the undergrowth and joined him.

The pig hung by one leg, twisting and squealing but unable to get down. The noose had wrapped itself around its upper leg and its limbs were splayed about with little dignity. Survival was never pretty, but this pig would help save three lives. It wasn't a big porker like you would find on a farm – it was somewhere between the size of a cat and a medium-sized dog, covered in brown, bristly hair.

Beck didn't take time to pause and admire his handiwork. He owed the pig a quick death and so he just walked up to it without stopping, spear gripped in both hands, raised over his shoulder. Without breaking step he thrust it into the pig's body, just behind the left front leg, right where the heart would be.

He had once been given an injection by a trainee nurse, who had been so determined not to cause any pain that it seemed to take about half an hour and was excruciatingly painful. A much more experienced nurse had said that the way to do it without pain was just jab the needle in and out, in half a second, before the body even realised what was happening to it.

Beck took the same attitude when killing an animal with a knife. The blade was sharp and pointed and it slid cleanly into the pig's flesh. He knew enough animal anatomy to avoid any bone that would divert the blade and cause the creature an extra moment's suffering. Hot blood spurted from the wound over his hands, and he felt the animal's tremors vibrate down the shaft for half a second. And then the pig just *stopped,* all life gone from it in an instant.

That was when he realised he hadn't even been breathing for the last thirty seconds. He puffed out and took some deep, slow breaths to slow his pounding heart. Job done.

"Right," he said with a sigh of satisfaction. "Let's see how Jian's doing."

He cut the pig down and hefted it over his shoulder, and they set off.

They had left Jian putting the camp together, and Beck could hear the fire crackling away.

"Got dinner...!" he called happily as they emerged onto the flat ground by the pool. And then the smile slowly faded from his face. Jian was slumped, motionless, on the ground beside the blazing fire.

CHAPTER 32

"Jian!"

Beck dumped the pig and ran forward. Jian moved slightly and groaned. Together, Ju-Long and Beck helped him sit up. There was the usual hiss of pain as Jian clutched at his wrist.

"I am sorry ... I felt faint ..."

"Don't apologise," Ju-Long said immediately. "You are injured. You shouldn't even be trying to set the camp up. We can ..."

And then she looked around the camp. Then stopped talking.

"... do absolutely nothing," Beck finished.

He had already seen the fire, but he hadn't had time to appreciate it. Jian had arranged a circle of stones to contain the ashes and embers, and built it exactly as Beck would have, with layers of tinder, kindling and fuel. He must have done it all with one hand, one stick or stone at a time.

Then he had done what he could for the sleeping quarters. There was nowhere to build a platform here, but they needed to be off the ground, for comfort, and to keep away from insects. They also needed to avoid the cold soil sucking the warmth from their bodies as they slept. So, Jian had put three hammocks together with the last of the rope net. Beck had cut three rectangles of netting before starting the hunt. Jian had fixed a piece of wood at each end to hold them apart and make sure they didn't just fold up on whoever was sleeping in them. With one hand, he had somehow managed to tie them up in the trees, ready for use. Beck was amazed.

The water bank looked like it was also in full production. They had brought every bottle they had from the old island, and while Ju-Long and Beck explored, Jian had found a big, empty two litre lemonade bottle washed up on the beach. The metal saucepan was bubbling over the fire with water from the pool – it needed at least five minutes from once it was properly boiling, to kill off any bugs. Once the water had cooled and settled, so that any bits could drop to the bottom of the pan, Jian could tip it into a bottle, throw away the bits, and start again.

Two bottles were already full and the next bottle in line was waiting.

"I thought," Jian said weakly, "while it was boiling, I should go back to the beach and mark the letters in the sand out. They will look very faint, on yellow sand. I used some of the dry seaweed and some stones to make them clearer. Then I started to feel tired, and I came back here, and I ..." He trailed off.

"You collapsed," Beck said. He wasn't sure whether to laugh or cry. "You've worn yourself out."

"I want to be useful," Jain said through his teeth.

"You *are* useful." Beck smiled. "But no one's useful if they work themselves into the ground. You must rest now."

"How is your arm?" Ju-Long asked.

"It is ... strange." Jian looked down at his hand. "I know it hurts a lot. Sometimes I feel a lot of pain, sometimes I feel nothing at all – but I still know it is hurting."

Beck bit his lip. He wasn't a doctor but that did not sound good. If the body was telling you that you didn't hurt, when you knew full well you did – well, that sounded like shock. It was the body's way of quietly shutting itself down so as not to alarm you.

In extreme cases it could go all the way – you could quietly die and not even notice.

What did he know about treating shock? He ran through his memories. Unfortunately, all he could come up with sounded very simple but it wasn't helpful under the circumstances. Keep the patient warm and comfortable, and wait for the medics to arrive. Nothing about what to do if the medics weren't turning up any time soon.

"Thanks for everything, Jian – you've done great," he said. "But doctor's orders now are to sit back and enjoy watching us work. Right? Just keep as warm as you can and stop exhausting yourself."

Jian didn't have the strength to argue. Instead, he quietly sat by the fire with his head between his knees. Beck gave him a lingering sideways look that he didn't notice. The contrast between this Jian – tired, haggard, weak – and the Jian of old was worrying, even if you counted everything he had gone through.

They had to get Jian to a proper doctor – and they had no way of doing so. Beck turned his attention to helping Ju-Long.

Beck wanted all three hammocks to have roofs, with supports made of branches and flotsam, and palm fronds for a rainproof covering. It would be easier to make one big roof than three small ones. He remembered the hint of rain clouds below the horizon that he had seen earlier. It was impossible to know if the rain was coming, but it would be foolish not to take precautions.

With a bit of tweaking with where Jian had placed the hammocks, they found the best place. Two of the hammocks went one on top of the other, with enough space between them so that the body weight of the person on top didn't make it sag into the face of the person beneath. The third they tied to the same tree as the other two, and the other end to a tree a little further away.

Ju-Long tested the first one by climbing in. She swung herself experimentally from side to side, and one end promptly came away from the tree. She hit the ground on her back with a laugh forced out of her by the impact. Jian's knot had held but the rope had snapped.

"Better to find that out now than later!" Beck added, as they both laughed.

She clambered up and started to re-tie the rope round double.

"I can fix this, and sort out the others, and the shelter, if you try and help Jian, maybe?"

Beck knew the answer. Their last meal had been the oysters on the old island.

"A proper meal and rehydrating is what Jian – and all of us – need. I'm onto it," Beck promised.

He had a pig to skin. This was going to be messy.

CHAPTER 33

Beck did the butchering wearing just his shorts. He didn't want to walk around tomorrow in clothes that were stinking of pig's blood and guts.

The first thing was to remove its guts and its genitals, because those were the bits that already had a high bacteria count and would start to go off almost immediately, spreading poison to the rest of the flesh. He hung the body up by its hind legs, so that its feet were a little higher than his head; then, with the knife removed from the spear shaft, he carefully sliced along the centre line of the pig's stomach, back up towards its hind legs, taking care not to puncture the guts. They would be full of semi-digested food and faeces, with plenty of poisonous bacteria that it was best to keep contained. The butcher's smell grew ten times stronger. When he was about half way up to the legs, the intestines began to ooze from the gash, sliding out like heavy, slimy balloons. They plopped onto the ground between his feet as he continued cutting.

He reached into the cavity, took hold of the guts and pulled down. Everything slid out neatly. He felt around inside for the solid lumps that were the kidneys, which he pulled out one at a time and cut free. These he set aside separately on a piece of wood to keep them off the ground.

Meanwhile Ju-Long gathered all the guts and parts that Beck said they wouldn't need, and buried them in a hole away from their camp. Next, Beck severed the head, and last of all, he removed the animal's skin.

He knew there was a lot of good food going to waste here. A proper butcher could have done many things with the jowls and the skin for bacon and crackling. But his concern was to give himself and his friends a proper meal.

The whole process had taken the better part of an hour, and all three of them were ravenously hungry. It was fully dark outside the circle of light from the fire. At last Beck could take the body down, run a skewer through it, and balance the two ends over A-frames that Ju-Long had tied together on either side of the fire. Ju-Long and Jian held the kidneys on skewers over the flames to cook separately. As Beck rinsed himself down with water from the pool, the smell of roasting pork began to drift over the camp. It was rich and gamey and seemed to go past their noses straight to their stomachs. It said: *make me count. I am here to help save you.*

And when they finally did, slicing off cuts of meat from the carcass and taking great bites out of the kidneys, they felt new strength flowing into their bodies. The warm food in their stomachs pumped out energy that was soaked up by their tired bodies. And at the same time it was as if their bodies finally gave them permission to shut down for the night. They were saying: *right, you've done your bit, now sleep so that we can digest this nourishing food you've given us properly.*

And sleep they did. Beck just had time to settle into his hammock, and feel it swaying beneath him, and wonder when it would stop swinging...

Then suddenly it was much later. His eyes opened and he grunted. The fire was a mass of glowing embers. Something had woken him up but he wasn't sure what. For a horrible moment his sleepy brain jumbled its memories and he thought he was back on the old island, listening without realising it to dragons trampling their water collection.

Then Jian shouted out of the dark, from his hammock below Beck's. A moment's quiet, and then he began to talk instead, at a more normal volume but far too quickly. It was all in Chinese and Beck had no hope of following it. His voice rose and fell and caught in the back of his throat.

It did not sound good.

Beck swung himself out of his hammock and down to the ground.

"Jian? Are you all right?"

He heard Ju-Long ask the same question as she scrambled up from her own hammock. Jian's voice rose to a shout again, and then dropped back down, but still he babbled. Beck tried to peer into Jian's face. The other boy's eyes opened and stared at him, and suddenly Jian's good hand was clutching at Beck's shirt.

"Hand … my … hand …" He relapsed into gabbling, tossing his head from side to side.

"He is soaked with sweat," Ju-Long reported, resting her hand on his head.

His hand …

Beck gently took Jian's damaged hand and studied it as best he could in the moonlight. Jian whimpered and tried to tug his hand away, but Beck held on.

"Okay. I'm going to take the splint off. See if there's something I can do. Okay?"

But he hadn't bothered waiting for permission – he already had the first rope untied even as he spoke. A few moments later and the splint came away.

Beck's heart thudded in his chest.

They only had moonlight to see by, but still Beck could see the dark streaks in Jian's skin. They were clear to see beneath his bandage and ran up from his wrist towards his elbow. Beck cursed beneath his breath and started to unwrap the bandage, though he had guessed what he would find.

The whole hand was badly swollen, starting from the dragon bites, and the skin was dark. Bacteria in the dragon's saliva had got into his system, despite Beck's best efforts.

He squatted back on his haunches and groaned.

"His blood is poisoned," Ju-Long said quietly. He nodded, mutely. "It could spread through his whole body. And if it does –"

There was no point in soft-peddling this. Anyway, Jian seemed to have passed out again and wouldn't hear a word they said.

"It will kill him," Beck said heavily. "I know."

He had tried to sterilise the wound – he obviously hadn't done it well enough.

Or maybe he had done enough to buy Jian a few important hours. Maybe the older boy would have already died without Beck's treatment.

And now he was on course to die again, if they didn't do something. He knew what the something was.

"I've seen this," he said reluctantly, "once before." She looked at him with a mute question. "We – my parents and I – we were in this village in Indonesia. The day we arrived, there was this guy in a really bad way – fever and hallucinations, and his whole leg was almost black. A log had fallen on it and the cut had festered in the tropical heat. The same helicopter that flew us in, flew him back to the capital to hospital. Next time I saw him…" He looked her in the eyes. "He was better." And as she started to look relieved, he finished: "Minus one leg."

Her eyes went wider than he had ever seen them before.

"And that was a hospital," he pressed on. He had to keep talking. He knew what he was going to have to do, and he *so badly* didn't want to that he felt he had to persuade himself into it. "They had all the modern high grade multi-spectrum anti-biotics and the best treatment available – and they still had to amputate."

He looked down at Jian. The harsh fact was, some of the dragon bacteria had survived, and they had bred, and now they were nestling deep in Jian's wrist and spreading out into the rest of his system.

"So what chance do we have?" she asked quietly. He nodded.

"If we can't get the poison out of him then we have to remove him from the poison," he said simply. "This hand has to come off. It's the only way."

CHAPTER 34

Scritch. Scritch. Scritch.

When the sun came up, it looked down on a busy scene. When Beck had sterilised the wound the first time, he had cut a strip off Jian's trousers to use as a bandage. They were going to need more than one bandage now. He had shredded as many of their clothes – his and Jian's and Ju-Long's – as decency would allow. All their sleeves and legs were gone. Beck just prayed it was enough.

And now he was sharpening the knife for its ultimate test.

Jian hadn't regained consciousness, though he still mumbled under his breath. Ju-Long was alternately wiping the sweat from his face and supervising the boiling of the bandages.

Scritch. Scritch.

The only way to stop Jian's wrist killing the rest of his body was to remove it from the body. *Scritch. Scritch.* Then, maybe, his body's natural defences would have a chance against the bacteria that were left.

If there was an alternative, he honestly couldn't think of it, though he was wracking his brains and trying hard. It was the hardest decision he had ever made.

Was he just risking even more infection? Despite taking every precaution they could?

Maybe. But if they didn't do this, Jian would *definitely* die.

But would the shock of an operation without anaesthetic finish Jian off?

Possibly. But if they didn't do this, Jian would *definitely* die.

Wouldn't it cause Jian even more pain?

Certainly. But more pain was better than *definitely dying.*

Might rescue come first?

That was what actually made Beck pause and think. Rescue might arrive, whisk Jian away to a decent hospital...

Might arrive. But if they didn't do this, Jian would *definitely* die.

He had never been to a single scout medical talk that discussed field amputation. They would have to proceed based on what they did know. They both knew basic biology – enough to say there are two bones in the lower arm, and how they connect together – and they both knew basic first aid. Beck knew how to cut up an animal, and all mammals have basically the same skeleton, only varying in size and shape.

After that, they were on their own.

Ju-Long had thought she remembered hearing something about an American who had had to cut his own arm off. Beck knew the story.

"A guy called Aron Ralston," he had said as he continued nervously to sharpen the blade. *"A boulder fell on him when he was out hiking, miles from anyone else, and it trapped his arm. The only way he could get free before he died of thirst was to cut it off. But he only had a blunt knife and he knew it would never get through his bones, so had to break them first..."*

Fortunately his knife was sharper than Ralston's had been. No bones would need breaking.

They were almost ready to go.

Then Beck faltered.

"I can't do this, Ju-Long. I really can't."

Ju-Long reached out and held his hand.

"You can't alone – but together we can. Jian needs us to be strong if he is to live. Together we have to do this."

Beck looked away. He remembered his mother once telling him, *never give up, Beck. However desperate or dire the situation, keep going. Just keep going.*

He took one final deep breath and looked at Ju-Long.

"Together. OK. Let's save Jian's life. Put the tourniquet on."

Ju-Long nodded, and wrapped a piece of rope a couple of times around Jian's upper arm. She tied the ends together over a piece of wood, then twisted the wood so that the leverage pulled the tourniquet even tighter, biting into Jian's flesh. Almost immediately the arm above it started to grow red as blood pooled up, and the skin below the rope slowly turned pale. She used another piece of rope to fix the wood in position.

Last of all, Ju-Long squeezed a small length of wood into Jian's mouth, between his teeth. With what was about to happen, Jian might grind his teeth together so hard he could bite his tongue off. He needed something safe to chomp down on.

Beck had a sudden memory of Ju-Long as he had first met her, at a getting-to-know-you party before their ill-fated expedition. Intelligent and alert, smart in her Young Pioneers uniform, confident in the success of the trek because of all the badges she had earned for this and that. Well, she was still intelligent and alert, but her confidence came from somewhere else now. She had been in survival situations she had never dreamed of, and come through them because of her own inner strength and ability. She didn't need badges to know she was good.

They don't actually give badges for what I'm good at... he had said at the party. And now, neither of them would be getting a badge for what they were about to do.

"This is it," Beck said. He had to act quickly, before the loss of blood in the lower arm just added to the damage. They knelt either side of Jian's motionless form, tied firmly to the wooden frame they had put around him to hold him still. Ju-Long braced herself and pinned his shoulders down, one more defence in case he suddenly started to move.

Just below the elbow, Beck thought – that should do it. Well above the red marks. He bit his lip and took hold of Jian's arm, then put the edge of the blade to the skin, and began to cut. With a few deft flicks of his wrist, he drew the knife all around Jian's arm. Blood immediately welled up.

Even in his swoon, Jian began to moan and breathe heavily. Beck shut his ears and his mind to the sound, and kept cutting. His friend's flesh put up resistance, almost like warm rubber. A knife that wasn't as sharp as Beck's had made his would have had difficulty. But he kept at it, drawing the blade back and forth, until he felt it hit bone. It was the thicker of the two bones, the radius. He immediately switched the knife around in his hand so that the serrated blade was foremost, and began to saw.

Jian's mumbled, incoherent sounds didn't get any louder: Beck hoped that if pain was penetrating his unconscious mind, then it had peaked. He couldn't imagine hurting Jian *more*.

Jian began to twitch: arms and legs jerking at where he was bound to the frame. Ju-Long laid a damp strip of cloth on his head, and stroked his hair, and murmured reassurance in Chinese into his ear. Her voice shook a little but she kept it mostly level, with a massive effort. The noises and the movements didn't go down, but they didn't get worse either.

The sawing blade made a sound like slicing through soggy wood, and Beck had chopped enough wood to know the secret was to just keep going – firm, steady strokes, and a constant downwards pressure. And just like sawing wood, the sound grew higher and higher the further he got through. Then there was suddenly no resistance and the first bone was through. He switched again so that he could cut another couple of centimetres through flesh, while Jian's blood coated the blade and his hand. Then he switched blades again for the ulna.

He felt, rather than heard, the ulna go. He was through, and Jian's hand was only attached to the rest of him by a few centimetres of meat. And then they came away, and Jian's arm with it. The bite marks were dark cavities, homes of bacteria that would not be causing Jian any more harm.

"Done," he said quietly. Ju-Long had the first of the bandages ready to wrap around the stump. The fabric immediately soaked through with dark red blood.

Beck carried the severed arm to a small pit he had dug earlier. He laid the arm in it and scraped the soil back in to cover it, then rested several small stones on top of it as a safeguard against any small animals that might want to sniff it out for food.

The daylight had grown colder and greyer as he worked. Thunder suddenly rumbled through the treetops and he glanced up. The sky was completely covered by dark, roiling clouds.

Ju-Long wrapped as many bandages as she could around the stump, then tied the arm across Jian's chest.

"A wound like this should be elevated," she said. Her voice sounded almost detached, like someone had taken it from a parallel world where they hadn't just cut someone's arm off – a world where everything was normal. "It should be higher than the heart if possible. And we must protect him against shock."

Beck nodded. He certainly wasn't going to argue.

They lifted Jian back into his hammock and covered him up with the two other hammocks and as much extra netting as they could manage, without burying him altogether. It was the best thing they could do without proper blankets.

Beck slowly released the tourniquet and they both peered anxiously at the bandages, to see how the surgery would cope with the renewed blood flow. No blood dripped through.

"We must change these twice a day," Ju-Long said, still in that voice.

"We'll keep 'em boiling, then," Beck said. And suddenly he had to turn away. If he stayed looking at Jian then he would never be able to think of anything else.

Would Jian live? If he lived, would he understand why they had done it? How would he adjust to life –

Stop, Beck told himself. *Just stop.* Always remember this – he would have *died.* Anything else we did, anything at all, there's a way of coming back from. But not from dying.

He thrust his hands into his pockets and looked out to sea. He had dealt with another problem, that was all. To survive, to keep surviving, he had to shelve that problem in his head and move onto the next. The next thing to do, if they were to stay alive. Care for Jian. Find resources. Plan what to do if still no rescue came. How long would it be for Mr Zhou to realise they were missing? How far would he look...?

He sensed Ju-Long behind him, and then felt her hand rest gently on his shoulder. He reached up to cover it with his own and for a while they just stood silently.

They looked up as another burst of thunder sounded, louder than before. They both heard the familiar hiss, quiet at first, then growing louder and louder until they could barely hear themselves speak, as the rainclouds broke above them.

CHAPTER 35

Beck stood on the beach and let clean, fresh water sluice over him from the sky. It soaked into his clothes and plastered them to his body. He turned his face up and felt the grime, the sweat, and above all the salt of the last couple of days wash away from him. *Boy,* did that feel good. He ran his fingers through his hair, then held out his arms and turned slowly beneath the shower.

It was a tropical rain storm. The water was the same temperature as the first drops that might dribble out of the hot tap back home. Back home, that would be a disappointment but here, after the heat of the last few days it was like every drop was infused with a fresh energy that soaked into his body.

On the mainland, after the storm, the water that had soaked into the ground would soon turn into vapour and the glorious freshness would turn into a steam bath. Out here, though, the sea breeze would keep the air flowing and it would stay fresh.

But not as fresh as it was now, when every drop was immediately followed by a new one.

But this wasn't about him. He had a job to do.

With an armful of empty bottles, he walked along the beach until he saw what he had expected to see. The rain had recharged the island's water systems. The dry gullies were flowing with clean water and streams coursed down the beach. So much so that he could fill the bottles, and shake them hard to dislodge all the salt and gunge that had inevitably accrued on them, and pour it away and fill them again. Water, water, everywhere – a life enhancing resource, a gift, and theirs for the taking, safe to gulp down immediately without having to be boiled first.

But eventually he was out of excuses to stay out in the rain, so he turned and carried his fresh load back up to the camp.

"You are soaked!" Ju-Long exclaimed.

She was sheltering beneath the cover she had built over the hammocks, alongside Jian. The rain had put the fire out, but she and Jian were dry. Water dripped through the trees and ran down the V-shaped palm fronds above the hammocks. Of course, sheltering under trees during a thunderstorm wasn't generally wise, but there were a lot more trees around, and many of them were higher. Lightning took the easiest route to hit something, which meant it often hit whatever was highest. They were probably safe, Beck thought.

"I feel better, though. Has..." Beck bit his lip. He had been going to say "has he woken up?" but the question answered itself with one look, and he didn't need the tiny shake of her head. Jian no longer showed the signs of delirium and fever – but he no longer showed the signs of anything much. His pulse had been faint the last time Beck tried it. He had an image of it hanging on by the tiniest thread, as thin as spider web, which may or may not break under the slightest extra force.

"You should give it a go too," Beck suggested instead, as she came forward to take the bottles off him.

"You will catch a chill as it dries."

He shook his head.

"Warm weather, low air pressure. It'll dry off in no time." He tried a very faint smile, but it faded as he looked at Jian.

"How is he?"

She pulled a face.

"But breathing is better," she added

They crouched down on either side of Jian's hammock and Beck leaned his ear close to Jian's face. Yes, that did sound better. Each breath was going in and out more smoothly, not sounding like it was being dragged over the teeth of a saw.

But those breaths were very weak.

He took a bottle and dribbled some drops onto Jian's lips, just enough to moisten them, but not so much that it would just run down his chin. He tried a little more. Jian's lips parted slightly and the water ran in. Again Beck kept the flow to a bare minimum, not wanting to flood his mouth and choke him. Just enough that he could unconsciously swallow it, get it inside him without even knowing.

Jian's head moved and a long, low breath rattled in his throat. His eyes flickered and half opened.

"Beck?"

It was a half whisper, but it sounded like the older boy's normal voice, not the harsh, angry shouting of his delirium.

He tried to open his eyes a little further, then winced and closed them immediately. He was as encrusted with salt and dirt as Beck had been.

"Hang on," Beck said. "I'm going to pour water on your face..."

He trickled the rest of the bottle, first over Jian's eyes, then the rest of his features. Jian himself was able to lift his good hand, with assistance, and wipe it weakly away.

Ju-Long was at the ready with another bottle. She held it to Jian's mouth with one hand and with the other she helped lift his head up, so that he could drink it properly.

"How do you feel?" Beck asked once the bottle was empty.

Jian laid his head back, a faintly puzzled expression on his face.

"I...I cannot even say how I feel in my own language, let alone English. I...I think I'm in pain. I don't know. It is so weird. I remember...I remember...I was unwell, I think? I felt..."

He looked around.

"This is not where we ..." Another pause. "We moved to a new island. I was on the raft."

"That's right. Do you remember why we had to move?"

"The ... dragons? One of them bit me ..."

At that he tried to lift his injured arm. Ju-Long had tied it so that it couldn't move and he only looked vaguely puzzled when he felt resistance.

"May I have more water?" His voice grew even fainter. "I am very tired ..."

He managed to get through half a fresh bottle before his eyes closed and his head lolled. Beck gently pressed his finger against the tendon in his neck, where the carotid artery passed close beneath. It was the best place to feel even a weak pulse.

The pulse was steady. Steady was good, he told himself. Wasn't it?

He and Ju-Long looked at each other over Jian's still form.

"We will have to tell him," she pointed out.

"Yeah, but all in good time." He didn't want to say, *Let's see if he lives first ...*

"This Aron Ralston," she said after a pause. "He lived?"

"Yup. He's alive and well, but his piano playing days are behind him."

She scowled, and Beck remembered she did not always appreciate his sense of humour.

"While Jian is unconscious, I will change the bandages."

"I'll help you."

He lifted Jian's arm up while Ju-Long unwrapped the bandages. First she dripped water on them to soften the clotted blood, so that she could pull them away from Jian's skin. The end of Jian's arm was a mass of raw, red flesh and dried blood, and fresh blood dribbled out of the rough surface immediately the bandages were free. Jian had their freshly boiled replacements ready. She started to wrap – and then paused.

"Beck. Look."

Beck's spirits, which had been rising as if pulled up by a very thin thread, plummeted. The thread had snapped.

The red lines that showed the course of the dragon's infection were creeping up Jian's skin above the cut.

Were they there because the bacteria were still fighting Jian's immune system? And if so, were they winning or was Jian? It had been nearly twenty four hours since Jian got bitten. How far had the bacteria spread around his body in that time? How much damage had they done that he couldn't see?

In theory, with the source of the infection removed, Jian's body should be able to fight back and defeat them. But Jian's body was hardly in the best shape. It might simply lack the strength.

If those lines were spreading, Jian could still die. Or Beck would have to amputate even higher. And that might just weaken Jian so much that he would die anyway.

Where was their rescue? When would anyone miss them?

CHAPTER 36

The rain let up eventually. Beck and Ju-Long had both drunk their fill of clean water, and refilled the bottles several times. They sat in tense silence and continued to moisten Jian's lips as often as they could, getting water slowly into him, drop by drop. They said nothing – there was nothing to say.

For breakfast they nibbled on some cold pork. They had left it on its skewer over the fire during the night so that the smoke would keep away any insects that might have felt like sharing their meal. Then they had brought it under the shelter with them when the sky opened.

Feeding Jian was out of the question without him waking up, which he didn't do. Beck felt his pulse frequently. It stayed steady. Beck was unsure if that meant he wasn't getting any worse, or that he was improving. Sometimes Beck lifted an eyelid with his thumb, and saw how Jian's pupil immediately contracted in the daylight. So, that meant his brain was functioning. But if Jian had had any kind of consciousness, there would have been resistance in the eyelid when it was lifted up. And there was none, which meant Jian was well and truly unconscious. Beck could only hope and pray that deep down, Jian's body was gathering strength that would eventually burst out into the rest of him.

Even after the rain had stopped, they stayed under the shelter with their injured friend. Maybe Jian didn't know they were there, with his conscious mind. But his unconscious mind could still register their presence, Beck thought. The pair of them were sending a signal: *You are not alone. We are here for you. We want you back.*

The woods around them were alive with the sound of dripping water. *Drip, drip, drip.* It was a cold, dull sound. The sky was still clouded over and the island seemed grey and lifeless.

Beck felt the same. He knew they were running out of options and he felt sick inside and it wasn't just from hunger.

Come on, Beck. Be positive. Contribute. Make a change. That's how you stay ahead of any dark cloud that might be chasing your thoughts.

"I'll get the fire going again," Beck said out of the blue. Ju-Long nodded. Activity, warmth – those would lift the spirits. And Beck had found it was a universal rule that a good fire could banish the gloom, inside and outside your head.

And when he had done that, he thought, he would see what they could do to upgrade their shelter into something a bit more weatherproof. And catch more food – no point in going hungry on a well-stocked island like this. And increase the signal too – make it into something that even the blindest lookout sailor couldn't miss. Just *keep busy.*

They had a supply of kindling and tinder with them, kept out of the rain. Beck used his hands to scrape the sodden heap of ashes and charred fragments out of the fire circle, then started to build a fresh pile.

Drip, drip, drip.

Thwack, thwack.

He paused, his head cocked. Had he heard –

Drip, drip, drip.

No. He started again.

Thwack.

"Beck –" Ju-Long too had paused what she was doing, a bottle halfway to Jian's lips.

"I thought I heard –"

Thwack, thwack, thwack.

"It's a helicopter!"

Beck leapt to his feet, turning a circle where he stood as he stared up through the leaf canopy. All he could see was the grey blur of the clouds above them.

He broke into a run, pelting his way through leaves and branches that seemed to conspire to hold him back – whipping at his face, snatching at his feet, until he had to force himself to go slower, or risk a broken ankle or poked-out eye.

He burst out onto the beach and gazed frantically around. There was no sign of a helicopter. They had built a signal beacon before the hunt the day before. It stood where they had left it. The letters that Jian had picked out in the sand had washed away, but their outlines were still shown by the dead weed and stones. Beck made a mental note that he would have to re-mark them. But, first things first.

Thwack, thwack…

Had it got louder? Quieter? Nearer? Further away?

He looked up at the clouds again. It was impossible to say how high they were. There was nothing for the eye to fix on. They could be low down, with the helicopter only just above them. Easy to see with nothing in the way, but now completely obscured.

Was it worth lighting the fire for? He might just be wasting a good blaze. But the smoke might rise above the clouds, or the helicopter might come down lower. It might actually be looking for them, so the crew would be keeping an extra close watch.

Put that way, there was no question. Beck pulled the protecting fronds away and struck his fire steel at the tinder.

Come on, come on…

The fronds had done their job – the pile was dry despite the rainstorm. Sparks settled onto the bone dry leaves at the base of the pile. Beck pouted his lips and blew gently on it. The sparks turned to little glow-worms that ran along the surface of the leaves and disappeared into the depths of the pile.

Thwack, thwack.

"Don't go!" he shouted, uselessly, at the sky. "Just hang on..."

Crack.

Something in the pile had caught. A few moments later, the first tendrils of flame began to poke through the gaps in the pile, like shy little animals nervously emerging from their burrows, not certain if it was safe. The air above the fire began to shimmer with warmth.

Beck ran up to the treeline and came back with a handful of wet leaves. He didn't want the fire to burn too clearly. He wanted smoke, and in the absence of flip-flops, wet leaves were the next best thing. He dumped the leaves onto the pile and ran back for a second load.

The flames had vanished. Had he just put the fire out? He held his hand flat above the pile, holding his breath until he felt the distinct touch of hot air on his palm. He snatched it away and waited for smoke to show.

That was more like it! Dark grey streams began to rise up from the beacon. He added more leaves and quickly stepped aside as the wind changed direction and the smoke swung round into his face. More leaves. It was turning into a decent, dark signal.

Thwack, thwack.

Was it quieter? Was it going away? He desperately followed the path of the smoke upwards with his eyes.

But then, silence. The helicopter must have gone.

Beck screamed into the empty sky, with all his might, in desperation.

"*Aaarrrgh!*"

CHAPTER 37

Beck bit his lip and slowly, deliberately, ground his heel into the sand. He felt tears welling up inside his eyes.

Then a small movement snagged the corner of his eye and he glanced up. The helicopter had dropped below the clouds. It was square and angular, the kind Beck associated with the military, painted white with smart red and blue stripes. Before they left port on *Dolphin*, Beck had seen a pair of motor boats in similar colours which Jian had said belonged to the Chinese coast guard. Its landing lights were like the burning eyes of a metal dragon flying purposefully straight at the island. Now he could hear it clearly. The sound of its engine has changed from a *thwack* to a full-throated, steady roar that shook Beck's bones.

Beck whooped and ran down to the waves, waving his hands above his head.

"Over here! Over here!"

The helicopter drew closer. Beck could see the helmeted shapes of the pilot and co-pilot in the cockpit.

It flew straight overhead, so close that Beck could read the numbers of its belly without difficulty. His spirits plummeted. They were flying by?

"No!" he bellowed. "*No!* Come here, come down here..."

But it was merely turning around in a wide circle. It came lower and slowed as its wheels folded down, and then it settled onto the beach between sea and trees, rotors whipping up a hurricane of sand and spray that made Beck flinch and cover his face.

The side door slid open and a pair of men in flight kit and helmets leapt out. They ran towards Beck and he finally lowered his arms.

The first man had a huge beam on his face as he spoke rapidly to Beck.

"Ah. Uh. Do you speak English…?" Beck asked hopefully. But suddenly Ju-Long was at his side. She spoke quickly to them and pointed towards the trees. The men frowned and nodded, and ran on, gesturing that Ju-Long and Beck should follow.

"He said," Ju-Long said between breaths as they ran, picking their way through the trees, "that they caught the signal from the radar reflector…"

Beck laughed and kept running until they were at the camp.

The men hurried forward and knelt by Jian's still form. One of them leaned over to lift an eyelid – and only then did he noticed the bandaged stump of Jian's arm. Then the leader spoke a few abrupt words to the other, who turned and pelted back towards the helicopter.

"He has gone to get the medical kit," Ju-Long whispered. Beck nodded. The remaining man felt for Jian's pulse in his neck, then took his hand and felt at the wrist. Beck's blood ran cold as he let go, and Jian's wrist flopped lifelessly to the ground.

The man pulled his helmet off and rested an ear against Jian's chest. Then he pulled himself up and placed the heel of one hand against Jian's breastbone. He put the other hand on top of it, laced his fingers together, and pushed down hard with straight arms.

Beck felt his eyes fill with tears as he stared at his friend's still shape.

"Oh, no… please… no…"

The other man was back, carrying a rugged green case. He knelt and threw it open while the first man changed tactic.

He tilted Jian's head back, pinched his nose shut and breathed directly into his mouth. The second man tore a plastic package open and produced a syringe the size of a bicycle pump with a needle that looked as sharp as Beck's knife. The first man used a pair of scissors to cut Jian's shirt open; Beck couldn't watch as the second man tapped the needle to clear it of bubbles, paused a moment and then plunged it into Jian's chest.

CHAPTER 38

"Time to get you home, Beck."

Beck had Skyped Al, back in London. He had given Al the full account of everything that had happened since *Dolphin* cast off from its quay a week earlier. It had been a long call, full of emotion for both of them.

"I *am* coming home, Al ..." Beck mumbled meekly. He shuffled forward one more step in the queue towards the security check and the Departures lounge of Macau International Airport.

"Will your uncle be meeting you in London?" Ju-Long asked. She was determined to accompany him as far as she could. She had even come with him in the taxi. He looked sadly at her – or not so much at her, as at the absence of Jian next to her. They hadn't known each other long, but by the end they had definitely been three friends. And now back to two.

He answered Ju-Long's question.

"He will. I expect he'll have the child locks on so I can't get out of the car, and then he'll personally escort me up to my room and lock the door so it's physically impossible for me to go off anywhere without him."

He saw the slight look of uncertainty that hovered over her face.

"Yes, that was a Beck joke," he said quickly. She smiled in relief. "But look at it from his point of view. He sent me to China in the first place because he thought it would keep me out of trouble. No more faking my death or anything."

"You did not get into trouble. Trouble came to you. The typhoon was not your fault. Everything that happened afterwards came from that. Everyone knows that."

The medical experts called in by Mr Zhou had been very clear that amputation had been the only way to give Jian even a ghost of a chance, and they would have done the same in Beck's place. The older man's understanding over what Beck had done to his son was overwhelming.

"I hope they do." He pursed his lips and puffed his cheeks out. That damn typhoon. It had caused the landslide that trapped Mr Zhou and the others, and it had shifted the sandbanks so that *Dolphin* ran aground. "I guess nature doesn't care. It just does what it does."

Ju-Long nodded softly. They slid forward another couple of paces.

"What will your uncle do then? Confine you to England?" she asked.

He pulled a weak smile.

"Maybe that's the best thing."

"Beck! We found you!"

The crowd parted as Jian came barrelling through, propelled aggressively in his wheelchair by his father. Both had huge smiles plastered to their faces.

"They let you out!" Beck exclaimed in delight.

The hospital had put up a fight, and who could blame them? They had a patient recovering from severe blood poisoning and an amateur amputation. He had just gone into cardiac arrest when the helicopter arrived. Watching the two men saving his life – compressing his chest, blowing air into his lungs, injecting adrenaline directly into his heart and then going back to CPR – had been the longest twenty minutes of Beck's life.

So, of course the doctors had wanted to hang onto him for as long as they could. Beck had already said goodbye to Jian at the hospital and Mr Zhou at home, so honour was satisfied – but he had really missed seeing them for this last bit.

Jian waved the question away like it was a fly buzzing around his face.

"If they had not, I would have walked."

He still looked tired, and Beck knew the wheelchair was just to keep him from overtaxing his body – nothing to do with his ability to walk. But there was colour in his face and a light in his eyes, and Beck knew his friend would be okay.

And then he saw, to his surprise, that Jian had two hands again.

"Oh. This." Jian lifted the arm up and Beck could see that it was of course a prosthetic – moulded plastic, coloured to match his skin. "This is to help them get my measurements. Eventually they say I will get a new arm and hand that will respond to my thoughts. Chinese science and medicine!"

"Waterproof, I hope?" Beck said with a grin, thinking of his friend's passion for sailing.

"Oh, yes! And able to pull on a rope."

"Well..." Beck couldn't take the grin off his face. "You're an amazing guy, Jian, you know that?" And the three of them hugged each other tight.

No survivor makes easy choices; the choice he had made had been the toughest of his life. Yet he knew that people with disabilities could go on to do incredible things with great determination in their lives. Beck knew Jian would be one of those inspirations.

The line moved a bit further forward. Another thirty seconds, and Beck would be at the barriers.

"Well..."

He got a final hug from Ju-Long, and shook hands with Mr Zhou once more.

"Thank you, Beck," Mr Zhou said sincerely. "Thank you. You will always be welcome back here."

"I will come back real soon," Beck promised.

"We will try to book some good weather," Jian promised. Beck laughed, and turned to hand his passport and boarding pass to the security man.

It was time to go home.

Survival Tips

HOW TO STAY ALIVE ON A DESERT ISLAND

HOW TO SPLINT A BROKEN BONE – LEG OR ARM

Due to pollution, it seems that every coastline has at least some polystyrene on it. When you are stranded with someone who has a broken bone you can use this sad fact to your advantage. Take some polystyrene and three pieces of drift wood, big enough to support the break, and cut the polystyrene into thin, flat lengths, the same length as the driftwood.

When a bone breaks, muscles around the bone contract to try and protect it. Unfortunately, this makes it harder to reset the bone; unless the bone is reset the broken ends could grind together and move around causing damage to the flesh, nerves and blood vessels.

To reset the bone, cut three short lengths of rope and lay them out placing the drift wood perpendicularly on top. Lay the polystyrene on top of the driftwood and then lay the broken limb on top of the polystyrene. The polystyrene is handy as it will stop the skin chafing against the wood. Now comes the painful bit, two people must pull the limb gently in opposite directions to set the bone in place. Feel the break as you pull; you should feel a shift under the skin as the bones pop back into place. Once this happens, quickly wrap the limb in the splint, sandwiching polystyrene between the break and the driftwood, before tying it together with rope. The knots must be tight enough to hold the splint in place, but loose enough to maintain the blood flow around the break.

FINDING DRINKING WATER

When you're stranded on a desert island the number one priority must be finding drinking water. It may seem like you are surrounded by the stuff, but drinking sea water is probably the worst thing you could do. The salt in the water will send your kidneys into overdrive, draw all the water out of your tissues and make you even worse than before. You should always try to find running water as water that has pooled will be stagnant and will be teeming with bacteria from animals and other debris. If you can't find any rivers or streams, look around the cliffs as these places will often hold small rock springs. You can find these by looking for vegetation on or under the cliffs and following faults in the cliff face.

These springs may only be a tiny trickle of water, but you can collect this water using a rope and a water bottle (or whatever vessel you can get your hands on). First, anchor the bottle into the ground. Dig a hole into the sand or gravel or if this isn't an option prop it up with some rocks. Now, find a way to attach your rope to the trickle on the cliff face. If the stream is in a fault in the cliff you can wedge it in there, if there is a ridge on the cliff try to use stones to anchor the rope. Cut the rope so that it is just long enough to dangle inside the mouth of the water bottle. Hopefully the water should now be trickling down your rope instead of the rock face. The surface tension in the water makes it cling to the fibres and drop by drop, collect in the water bottle.

SHELTER

First of all, use your surroundings. Look for fallen trees or anything that could give you some shelter from the elements. Do bear in mind that if there is a thunderstorm the last place you want to be is under a tree.

When establishing somewhere to sleep, it's important that you don't sleep directly on the ground. Sleeping on the cold ground will suck all the warmth from your body. You also want to keep away from any creepy-crawlies that could bite you in your sleep.

Try to find or build some kind of platform to sleep on. Some rock types, like granite, radiate heat at the end of the day so sleeping near or on that could provide you with some much needed heat. If you can't build a platform at least build a mattress of ferns, pines and leaves to provide a little insulation.

MAKING A BEACON

To improve your chances of rescue, you have to make a beacon. Find the best point of visibility on the island, it needs to be high up and close to the shore to be able to attract both ships and helicopters.

To build the beacon, first make a tripod. Tie two planks of wood together at one end using a hitch knot and wrap the rope around the knot several times. Now wedge a third plank in between the first two and tie that in place as well.

Stand the tripod up and make a platform about halfway up. You can do this by using shorter pieces of wood to make a triangle between the tripod legs that will enable you to lay more pieces of wood across it.

Now you must build the fire. Use pieces of dry bark or leaves as tinder and lay the kindling on top, making sure that air can circulate around the tinder. Once you have a fire going, look for any artificial or plastic materials that may have washed up on the shore as these will create thick, acrid smoke that will easily attract attention.

Above all, remember: never, ever give up!

Bear Grylls has become known around the world as one of the most recognized faces of survival and outdoor adventure. His journey to this acclaim started in the UK, where his late father taught him to climb and sail.

Trained from a young age in martial arts, Bear went on to spend three years as a soldier in the British Special Forces, serving with 21 SAS. It was here that he perfected many of the skills that his fans all over the world enjoy watching him pit against mother-nature.

His popular survival TV shows include 'Man Vs Wild' and 'Born Survivor' which became one of the most watched programmes on the planet with an estimated audience of 1.2 billion. He has also hosted the hit adventure show 'Running Wild' on NBC, where he takes some of the world's best known movie stars on incredible adventures. Most recently US President Barrack Obama asked to appear on the show for a worldwide 'Running Wild Special'.

Bear is currently the youngest ever Chief Scout to the UK Scout Association and is an honorary Colonel to the Royal Marine Commandos.

He has authored 22 books, including the international number one Bestselling autobiography: *Mud, Sweat & Tears* and his hugely popular titles *Survival Guide for Life* and *True Grit*, a bestselling novel *Ghost Flight* and his *Mission Survival* fiction books which have sold over 4 million copies in China alone.

If you'd like to know more, please visit Bear's website, www.beargrylls.com where you can sign up for his most recent news, or follow him on Twitter, @BearGrylls, or on Facebook.

Also in this series

34087349R00100

Printed in Great Britain
by Amazon